PRETTY FILTHY LIES

Jeana E. Mann

Thanks to all my friends for their support.

Chapter 1

Dakota

A MIX OF excitement and trepidation stirred butterflies to flight in my stomach as I stood on the sidewalk in front of Infinity Enterprises. I blamed the internal fluttering on the hot sex I'd just had in the limousine and the thought of a fresh beginning in a life fraught with tragic endings. The man at my side was an integral part of my anxiety. Samuel Seaforth, corporate predator and ruthless businessman, was the most complicated, infuriating male I'd ever met. He was also my boss and my ex-husband.

I cast a glance at him, tall, cool, and imposing in a charcoal suit jacket over a crisp white dress shirt and black trousers. Overcome with shyness, I fought the blush threatening to color my cheeks at the way he'd ravaged my body, the way he'd touched me, claimed me. He still wanted me, in spite of my epic flaws, poor decisions, and our painful history. Ten years ago, I'd broken his heart and betrayed us both. The game had changed this morning. He hadn't made any promises, hadn't said he loved me, but he had said he was willing to try. I needed a miracle in my life, and this was it.

We stood in front of a resplendent, three-story, Greek revival mansion. I hesitated, momentarily overwhelmed by the brilliant white columns lining the front and sides. The residence had been transformed into offices, but traces of its past life lingered in the meticulous gardens and the outbuildings beyond. Had Sam done the renovation? As teenagers, he'd been consumed with architecture and revitalizing old buildings. Did that desire still linger, to restore beauty to forgotten and neglected things? This glimmer of the boy from my past pleased me.

Green eyes met mine. My knees dissolved at the memory of his big hands up my skirt. The wind surged and ruffled his blond hair. He shoved a distracted hand through it, cell phone always at his ear.

"Dakota? Today, please." He jerked his chin toward the entrance before continuing the conversation with one of his minions. Whatever intimacy we'd shared in the car dissipated. My forehead tightened in a frown. He scowled back and barked into the phone. "Did I ask for you to forward those reports? No. I didn't. It's not what I wanted. If you'd listened to my instructions, you would have known that. You'll have to call Mr. Takashima and apologize for the error."

So demanding, my Samuel. Good thing he was hot. Otherwise, he'd just be an irritating ass. His hand rested on the curve of my hip, urging me forward. A thrill zinged along my side, radiating from his touch. Still high from the sex, I passed through the double entrance doors and wide foyer, conscious of his gaze on my backside. Crystal chandeliers sparkled overhead. I trailed fingertips over the smooth polished bannister of the sweeping staircase, climbing upward.

Voices and laughter floated down to us. At the top of the steps, Sam opened a set of French doors into what must have once been a ballroom but now contained a series of office cubicles. Muted tones of gray and gold covered the walls and furnishings, anchored by black details. Classic, understated, elegant. Sam's taste touched every element.

A woman rushed forward, pen and paper in hand, a worried frown on her middle-aged features. Silence replaced the laughter, followed by the sound of scurrying footsteps. Sam swept an assessing gaze around the room. The woman fell into step with us. She was petite and well groomed, wearing a pink blazer and skirt, the picture of conservative good taste.

"Mr. Seaforth, I'm so sorry. We weren't expecting you," she stammered.

"Obviously," he said.

"Can I get you or your guest anything?"

It took a second before I realized she meant me. I lifted an eyebrow at Samuel. Apparently, he hadn't informed his staff I was coming onboard.

"Mrs. Cantrell, this is Ms. Atwell. She's not my guest." He unbuttoned his jacket and continued pacing toward the end of the room. The woman trotted beside us in tiny, furious steps, heels clicking on the polished hardwood. "She'll be acting as a consultant on the MacGruder acquisition. Get her an office and anything else she needs."

He stopped at the end of the room. The heavy walnut door in front of us bore a brass plaque with *Samuel Seaforth, C.E.O.* engraved upon it in elegant script. He opened it and stepped aside to let me enter. The room boasted coffered ceilings, burled walnut paneling, and intricate plaster moldings. The biggest mirror I'd ever seen, gilt-framed and ostentatious, spanned the wall beside his desk. Beyond the lead-paned windows, a profusion of colorful flowers brightened an emerald green lawn.

"You've got a ton of messages," Mrs. Cantrell said. "Mr. Takashima called twice."

"I've already spoken with him." Sam shrugged out of his jacket and placed it on a hanger inside the closet near the door. "Anything else?"

"Mr. MacGruder called too, and--" She hesitated, blinking hazel eyes from

Sam to me and back again. "Your father called. He said it was important."

At the mention of Maxwell Seaforth, a chill swept through the room in spite of the warm sun outside the tall windows. Every time I heard his name, unpleasant memories wrenched my insides. I couldn't separate my former father-in-law from the most devastating mistake I'd ever made. We would forever be entangled--me, Mr. Seaforth, and Sam.

Sam's jaw flexed and his broad shoulders went rigid beneath his starched dress shirt, where my hands had been less than fifteen minutes earlier inside his limousine.

"Did he say what he wanted?" His voice carried an undercurrent of tension.

"No. Only that it was imperative you call him back." Her face fell, marred with lines of distress. "I'm sorry. I should have insisted on more information."

"It's okay." He took a seat in the luxurious leather chair behind an expansive desk and powered on his desktop computer. "That's all, Mrs. Cantrell."

The door closed behind her with a muted click. I stood in front of his desk and shifted from foot to foot. Sam leaned back in his chair and regarded me in silence for so long that my palms began to sweat. I lifted my chin, stared back, and refused to let him see my uncertainty. What lurked behind those beautiful irises? I had so many unanswered questions, but he seemed unwilling to offer any answers.

"Do you have something for me to do, or are you just going to let me stand here all day?" I asked, impatience getting the best of me. "It seems like a waste of salary, but it's your money, I guess."

His full mouth twitched with the faintest of smiles. "Standing there is nice." The way his gaze roved over my lips and eyes had my toes curling inside my shoes. His voice lowered to a deep growl. "Naked would be better."

Desire prickled over my skin at the wanton undercurrent in his words. "What would Mrs. Cantrell say?" I liked seeing him this way, knowing he wanted me.

"She'd be shocked."

We shared a smile. A hundred new questions raced through my mind. Why had he changed his mind? Why was he giving us another chance? Or was this simply nostalgia and temporary? The niggling insecurities tempered my euphoria.

"You don't need me here, Sam. You've got a huge staff to help you," I said in a low, quiet voice. "Why am I really here?"

"I do need you. For reasons I'd rather not go into right now." He leaned forward, elbows on the desk, fingers steepled in front of him. "There are things you don't know. The game has changed." Fire sparked in his eyes, a predatory gleam mixed with the sunlight from the windows. "Go ahead and take a seat." He nodded at the leather chair in front of his desk. "Before we dive in, we need to get a few ground rules in place."

"Okay." I licked my lips, mouth gone dry. His ominous tone erased my optimism and replaced it with apprehension. I lifted a hand to my neck, searching for the gold chain holding my wedding ring as I always did when I was nervous, and found nothing. My hand dropped to my side. I'd searched my apartment up and down for it to no avail.

"What happened in the limo, it was--" The line of his jaw tightened, and his voice trailed away. "I don't want to lead you on or give you false hope for something more, because I'm not ready for that." A knot began to tighten in my gut. All my shiny new hopes plummeted to the floor. "I want to trust you, but I can't. Not yet. Maybe not ever." I stared at my toes and tried to hide my disappointment. "You have to earn it back."

"I understand." I forced neutrality into my tone when I wanted to groan in despair. He came around to the front of the desk and sat on the edge, his spread knees on either side of mine. The gravity of his gaze renewed the guilt over everything I'd done, all the ways I'd betrayed his trust, our love. "I wouldn't expect anything less from you." I let my focus drop to my lap where my clasped hands rested, knuckles white with tension.

He tipped my chin up with his index finger until our eyes met. "What you did, coming to me with the contract and the check, it took guts. I respect that. It made me think there might be a chance for us." His lips twitched in the tiniest of smiles, sending my heart into an erratic dance. He brushed the pad of his thumb along the seam of my mouth. "Don't disappoint me, Dakota."

"I won't," I whispered. All I wanted was an opportunity to make things right, to prove how much I loved him, to repair all the damage I'd done.

"Mr. Seaforth? You have a call on line four. Alessandro Reyes." Mrs. Cantrell's disembodied voice came over the intercom. He stood and returned to his chair, widening the distance between us. "Do you want me to take a message?"

"No. I'll take it. Give me a minute." He waited for her to disconnect before he spoke to me again. "Are we good here, Dakota?"

"Yes, we're good." Did I have any other choice? Once again, he held all the cards in our game of love and wits. My only chance for reconciliation rested in rebuilding the foundation of our relationship, the one I'd obliterated with my betrayal. Hope unfurled inside me once again, and I picked up the challenge Samuel offered. I liked to win, and no matter how long it took, I would make this right.

Chapter 2

Sam

I FOUND IT hard to concentrate on work, knowing Dakota was under the same roof. The hour hand circled the clock on my desk while I moved through conference calls and meetings, ticking away the time until I could see her again. The past few weeks had been hell without her. I wanted so desperately to believe in her, to think we might be able to make a go of things, but I wasn't optimistic. Once upon a time, I'd had lofty dreams of picket fences and a cozy house filled with kids. But that had been before. Before Dakota's betrayal, before our divorce, before my father had become my enemy. Since then, my feet were rooted firmly on the ground, where they belonged. Life had taught me a few things. First and foremost? People didn't change.

The intercom buzzed, bringing me back to the present. "Your father is on line six," Mrs. Cantrell announced.

"Give him voice mail," I replied without hesitation. "Or take a message." My father was the primary source of my black outlook. Malcolm Seaforth was a cold-hearted, unforgiving tyrant who reveled in making others miserable for his personal entertainment.

"He's requesting a meeting."

"Pencil him in about fifteen minutes after hell freezes over." I turned my chair to face the window and gazed over the serenity of the garden below. The man never gave up. It was something father and son had in common. After what he'd done to Dakota, to me, to my mother, the way he'd made our lives miserable--I could never forgive him. I would spend the rest of my life making him atone for all the lies he'd told me. The pencil in my hand snapped in two as I thought of him.

A quick knock at the door preceded Beckett's entry. My best friend strode into the room, filling it with his tall, athletic frame. I swept the remnants of the pencil into the trashcan beside my desk while he eased into the chair across from me. He stretched his long legs out in front of him and clasped his hands on his lap.

"Good morning, counselor," I said.

"What's up?" he asked. His knee bounced with excess energy. "Are we on for drinks tonight?"

"Not tonight." I lowered my eyes to the report in front of me and smoothed a hand over it.

"Why not?" he asked with the same tone he used to cross-examine a witness on the stand. I knew from experience to keep my answers short and non-committal to prevent arousing his curiosity in matters I hoped to keep private.

"Busy." Becks was an all-around good guy, but sometimes he annoyed the hell out of me. He had a successful law practice and acted as chairman of the board at Infinity. It was a figurehead position, allowing me to control the direction of the business. I needed someone at the head of the company, someone I trusted, and Becks fit the bill. Not only was he a kick-ass divorce attorney, he was also shrewd and intelligent.

"Doing what?" He shifted in the chair, blue eyes blazing with interest. "Hot date?"

"No." I kept my gaze trained on the document, determined to remain stoic. "Business." Although he was a serial player himself, Becks had an infuriating fascination with my dedication to promiscuity. He dreamed about the day some girl claimed my heart and sent my self-control into a tailspin.

"Alright. Whatever. But I'm starting to worry about you, man. You've been in a funk for weeks now."

"I'm good." Relief washed over me as he stood and strode back to the door.

He paused with his hand on the doorknob. "Who's the skirt?" he asked, posing the question I'd been dreading. "Sexy chick? Brown hair?"

"That would be Ms. Atwell."

His eyes narrowed. "Ms. Atwell?" I sensed the cogs turning in his head as he put two and two together. A slow, incredulous smile spread over his face. "Your ex? Holy shit. Are you kidding me?"

Up to this moment, I'd been able to keep Dakota a secret from my friends. As far as they knew, she'd been a tragedy of my past and a blip on the radar of my present. Judging by the look on his face, he was thrilled by the complications presented by this turn of events.

"Is she the reason you're busy tonight?" His eyes lit with excitement. "Are you boning your ex-wife?"

"Don't start." I held up a hand to stop the teasing I knew was forthcoming. "She's here as a consultant. That's it."

"I thought you hated her. Or is this all a part of your wicked plan for retribution?" To my disappointment, he released the door and turned back to me. I groaned and steeled for the inquisition. "To make her pay?" He tapped a finger to his lips, feigning contemplation. "So you sleep with her, make her trust you, then *bam*, you jerk the rug from underneath her. Right?"

"You think I would do that?" Spoken aloud, the vendetta sounded cruel and pathetic, even for me. It was, however, pretty close to my original plan, before I'd known the truth about my father's part in Dakota's defection. Before I'd realized how much I missed her.

"You're a Seaforth. I think you'll do whatever it takes to get what you want." Beck's gaze met mine, challenging.

I twisted in my chair, uncomfortable under his all-too-knowing scrutiny. "Right. That's me. Take no prisoners." Was this the way everyone saw me? I swallowed down the sour taste in my mouth. It was one thing to overtake and disseminate a business, something entirely different to destroy a person. But that was what I did. Businesses were composed of people, and I annihilated businesses. I passed a hand across my brow, confused by the blurred lines of my morality.

"You are one ruthless son of a bitch." Becks clapped a hand on my shoulder. "Did I ever tell you that?"

I smiled halfheartedly and rose to walk him to the door. "Thanks."

"This Dakota, she must've really done a number on you." Emotion clouded his features as he regarded me. "I hope you know what you're doing, Sam."

An arrogance I didn't feel buoyed my reply. "Are you doubting me?"

"Hell no. You're my freaking idol, man." The tension in the room eased a little. "I'm just throwing this out there, so feel free to ignore it if you want. But I've seen you crush men without a backward glance. You've left dozens of women in your dust. So why are you hung up on ruining a girl who's already lost the game? It makes me wonder if you still have feelings for her."

"She means nothing to me," I said and opened the door. The moment the words left my lips, I cringed inside, recognizing the lie. It hung on the air between us, stagnant and accusing. I could tell myself she meant nothing, that her presence was only temporary, but saying the words aloud made me realize the truth. I wanted more. I wanted to believe in her. I wanted to make this permanent.

"I've got to meet this girl," he said. The gleam in his eyes set off warning bells in my head.

"No." I opened the door wider, banging my foot in the process. He passed over the threshold, his amusement growing at my distress. "I mean, not right now. She's in a meeting."

"Sure." By the smirk on Beckett's face, he didn't believe a word of it. "Later then. I've got a deposition in a bit anyway." As he moved out the door, he turned to walk backward and pointed at me. "You and me and Tucker, on the basketball court Wednesday. Don't forget."

Chapter 3

Dakota

MY TEMPORARY OFFICE was little more than a glorified closet with a French door leading onto the balcony adjoining Sam's office. Once I settled in, I stared through the glass at the green lawn dotted with spring blossoms and tried to corral my thoughts. Sam wanted to meet in a few hours to go over the research I'd done before quitting Harmony. All I wanted was to run my fingers through his hair and taste his lips on mine again.

Fantasies of Sam would only derail my productivity when I needed to be on top of my game. With a quick shake of my head to clear the cobwebs, I focused on reviewing the data I'd spent weeks compiling. I'd barely found my concentration when someone knocked on the door. A dark-haired young man poked his head into the room.

"Knock, knock," he said, breezing into the office, a crystal vase of white roses in hand. "I wanted to introduce myself before you got too busy."

I tore my gaze reluctantly from the monitor to regard him as he placed the bouquet on a table near the door. He rested his rear end on the corner of my desk and returned my perusal. He was small and slender with a crooked smile. A hint of guyliner defined bold gray eyes. The cut of his lemon yellow suit was impeccable, the color questionable. "I'm Xavier, with an X. Sam's assistant. And you would be Ms. Atwell." He lifted a well-groomed eyebrow, as if daring me to contradict him.

"Dakota, please." I extended a hand, and he shook it, his grasp warm and firm, confident. I immediately liked him.

"Sam asked me to check in on you. See if there's anything you might need." The way he spoke made me wonder if Sam had sent him at all or if this was some kind of personal fishing expedition. "He said to make sure you're comfortable during your stay."

"I'm good, thanks. Although...where can I get some coffee?" The thought of wandering the maze of hallways left me cold, and I'd given up my search after the first wrong turn. "Coffee is my lifeblood."

"Mine too. There's a coffee station around the corner. I'll show you. And there's a mini-fridge in the armoire." He gestured a manicured hand at the heavy Victorian piece against the far wall. "Just let me know what you want. I'll have it stocked. "

"Thanks." We stared at each other for another beat. He was handsome in a pretty, feminine kind of way. Hair slicked back. Eyebrows thick but perfectly groomed into twin wings. I tapped a finger on the keyboard, impatient to get back to work.

"You'll find everyone friendly around here," he said. "You're welcome to join us for lunch. We usually go to the café down the street or bring something back, and there's a kitchen downstairs."

"Thanks. I appreciate the invitation." The idea of lunch caused a nervous rumble in my belly. Would Sam expect me to wait for him? Should I stay in the office and work through? I thought our reconciliation would ease my insecurities.

Instead, it only fueled them. "I'm not sure..."

"No problem. I understand. Just throwing it out there."

An awkward silence fell between us.

"I really should get back to work." I cleared my throat and glanced at the computer.

"Of course," he said but didn't get up. He traced the edge of the desk calendar with a finger. "Have you known Sam long?" Calculating eyes blinked up to mine.

So, it was a fishing expedition. I debated the merits of truth versus secrets and decided to go with the truth. I'd been living with secrets long enough. The concept liberated the tension in my shoulders. "We met in high school."

"Shut the front door," he replied, genuine shock wiping away the curiosity. "Really? That long ago?"

"Yes." For some unknown reason, I found perverse pleasure in his surprise. "We were just recently reacquainted."

"Lucky you." His voice held a note of genuine awe. "Tell me, what was young Sammy like?" He leaned forward, body vibrating with curiosity. "Got any dirt?" His eyes gleamed, eager and bright. "I transferred here from the Chicago office. I've been his assistant for four years, and I know absolutely nothing about him. Aside from the work stuff. No one does."

The question caught me off guard. I leaned back in the chair, using a few seconds to gather my response. Sam had always been a private person. If he hadn't shared his past with his coworkers, there was a reason, and I wouldn't be the one to break his confidence. Never again.

"Well, that's Sam." I waved a hand dismissively. "Like I said, it's been a long time. We aren't really that close anymore." *Although we did screw in the car on the way over*, I added mentally with an inward smirk.

"I can respect that." He nodded and appeared satisfied with my answer. "Come on. I'll show you where the coffee is and let you get back to work."

* * *

With a cup of steaming java in my hand, I turned from the coffee station to find a dozen pairs of questioning eyes surrounding me. My new coworkers were a diverse group. Some looked barely old enough to hold a driver's license, fresh-faced and exuberant. Others seemed on the verge of a retirement home, stooped in posture with worldly wariness in their eyes. I had to wonder what Sam saw in them. I was certain each person possessed a unique quality, or he wouldn't waste his time with them.

"Hello?" I lifted my eyebrows in Xavier's direction. He shrugged one shoulder.

"This is Ms. Atwell," he announced to the group at large. "She's acting as a consultant for Mr. Seaforth." He made a dramatic pause. "They went to high school together."

The group shared a collective gasp. Then came a barrage of rapid-fire questions that left me breathless.

"Are you married?" asked a thin girl with freckles.

"Divorced," I replied.

"Kids?" queried an older man in a too-large suit. "We could use more family people around here."

"No." I set the coffee cup on the counter and braced a hand against it for stability against the inquisition.

Mrs. Cantrell came around the corner and vibrated to a stop at the sight of the crowd blocking the tiny alcove.

"What was he like when he was a kid?" This question came from a pretty brunette with a cherubic, round face. "Mr. Seaforth?"

"Um--" I cast a desperate glance at Xavier, hoping for an intervention, but it was Mrs. Cantrell who came to my rescue.

"I'm sorry to interrupt, Ms. Atwell, but Mr. Seaforth asked for an update on the information he requested." Our eyes met. I recognized her as an ally. She lifted her chin in acknowledgment.

"Right. Thank you," I said, giving her a genuine smile. "I'll get right on it."

The curious throng dissipated within seconds, and I let out an audible sigh of relief.

"They can be brutal," Mrs. Cantrell said. "But they're mostly harmless. You'll soon learn who you can and can't trust." She refilled her coffee cup and turned to follow me back through the corridor. "You're not the first, you know."

"I'm sorry?" Although I had no idea what she meant, heat rose in my cheeks.

"Of his *interns*." The emphasis she put on the word caused my forehead to furrow. "He likes pretty girls. Brunettes mostly." She stirred her coffee with the small plastic straw before dropping it into a nearby trashcan. "None of them lasted very long."

"Oh?" I wasn't sure whether to take this as a snide barb or a warning. The warm, fuzzy feelings of camaraderie fizzled away and left disappointment in their wake. It would've been nice to have a friend amid unfamiliar surroundings, but the turn of the conversation reminded me of two things. I was an outsider here, and I could trust no one.

"I don't mean to be rude." She touched my arm. Thankfully, we'd reached my door. "I just thought you should know. You seem like a nice person." She followed me into the office and watched as I returned to my desk.

"Thanks?" My disappointment lessened. I wasn't here to make friends. This wasn't high school. I was here for Samuel, to win back his trust, to repair our relationship, if that was even possible, and to do a job.

"I've offended you. I'm sorry." She lingered, watching me with shrewd interest.

"It's fine." I mustered a polite smile, not wanting to alienate her completely, but dialed back the enthusiasm. It would be helpful to keep her close until I figured out the pecking order of the office. "If you'll excuse me, I'm really very busy."

I thought she might leave, but she continued, offering information I didn't want or need to know. "Most of them were college interns. Three this year so far, not including you." Her gaze traveled over my face and figure, returning to meet my eyes. "You're a bit older than the others."

Just like that, all of my insecurities reared their ugly heads. I knew Sam hadn't been a monk since our divorce, but I liked to pretend he'd existed in a kind of suspended animation, waiting for me to come back. Jealousy prickled the skin along the back of my neck. At thirty years of age, I wasn't exactly a perky co-ed, but I wasn't a complete loser either. I straightened my shoulders and stared Mrs. Cantrell in the eyes. Determination strengthened my resolve. She wouldn't intimidate or berate me. And by my calculations, she was a few rungs lower on the ladder of power than me.

"Well," I said in a strong, quiet voice, "I'm not an intern, so please don't refer to me as one. I'm a consultant. And I can assure you I'm not like the others."

Chapter 4

Dakota

DESPITE MY GROWLING stomach, I worked through lunch, completely engrossed in my research. Two hours passed in a whirlwind of emails and Internet searches. When Sam strode into the room unannounced, I jerked and sat back in my chair with a startled gasp.

"Don't you ever knock?" I asked, biting back a smile of happiness at the sight of him.

"Nope." His lips twitched in a reciprocal show of appreciation. "Get your things. We're going out."

"I thought you needed this." I waved a hand at the computer screen, the cost projections, and the demographics. Everything was always an emergency with him--until it wasn't. I had yet to acclimate to his rapid change in priorities. "Like, yesterday."

"Bring it. We'll go over it on the drive." He turned and strode toward the door, buttoning his suit jacket on the way. I paused for a second to admire the way his trousers stretched over his lean hips, the indentation of muscle on either side of his ass. A quick glance over his shoulder allowed him to catch me in the act. One of his golden eyebrows lifted. I bit my lip and yanked my gaze back to the computer, embarrassment heating my face.

"I'm not done yet," I protested, even though the prospect of going anywhere with him caused my pulse to flutter.

"Dakota." It was one word. My name. Every time he said it, my knees disintegrated, along with my resolve.

"Okay. Fine." With a click of the mouse, I saved the information to a flash drive. "Give me a sec, Mr. Impatience."

He paused at the door, glancing at his watch, brows furrowed. "Meet me at the car." I groaned. He couldn't even wait here long enough for me to gather my belongings. "Five minutes," he warned, but his smile had returned.

When I exited the building, my heart leaped at the sight of Sam leaning against the passenger door of his car. He had one hand shoved into his pants pocket. The other held his cellphone to his ear. Our gazes met across the distance. How many times had he waited for me in this way when we were dating, when we were married? It had been years ago since the first time, but excitement pulsed through my veins, the very same way, as if it had been days and not a decade.

He raised his chin in greeting and stepped aside to open the passenger door for me. That was when I realized it was a red 911 Porsche. His Porsche. *The* Porsche. The same car he'd received for his eighteenth birthday. The car we'd made love in for the first time. Or at least a similar one. I froze in my tracks, overcome by the memories.

"Get in," he said at the same time he ended his call.

Recovering my composure, I slid into the seat, the black leather warm against my bare legs. He closed the door behind me then paced around the car to his side and folded his tall frame behind the wheel. I ran trembling fingertips over the stitching of the upholstery, unable to fathom this latest surprise.

"My real estate agent called. She's got an apartment for me to look at. I thought we could go over your info on the way." He cast a sideways glance at me while turning the key in the ignition.

The engine purred to life. The familiar vibration of the automobile had me dumbstruck. I watched Sam's long fingers grip the shifter and was immediately transported back to the past. For the briefest of seconds, I remembered what it felt like to be that girl, for us to be teenagers in love, oblivious to the oncoming disaster of our future.

"Where do you live now?" I asked through a haze of conflicting excitement and nostalgia, disconcerted to realize I didn't know this basic fact.

"I've been staying on the third floor of Infinity. He cast a second glance at me, eyes narrowed. "I own the building. I haven't converted it to offices yet."

"But your home office is still in Chicago, right?" My voice sounded tinny, far away. His big hand left the shifter long enough to fiddle with the radio before returning to the shifter. I swallowed against the thickness in my throat and remembered the way he'd pulled me over to the driver's seat with those hands, arranging my legs on either side of his thighs, pulling me onto him...

"For the time being." His thigh muscle contracted beneath his trousers as he pushed the clutch and downshifted. "I'm in the process of relocating everyone here. The cost of living in Laurel Falls is much more reasonable than Chicago."

"I had no idea." I struggled to carry on the conversation while more questions careened through my head. Why did he still have this car? Did he ever think about that day?

"Dakota?" His eyes rested on me as we waited at an intersection for the stoplight to change from red to green. "Are you listening?"

"Yes. No." I blinked away the fog. "I'm sorry, but is this the car?" He cocked his head slightly in question. "I mean, *the* car. You know?"

The left corner of his lips curled like a comma. His voice lowered, even deeper than normal. "Yes." My gaze flicked to his, finding it dark and enigmatic. "The same."

The apartment turned out to be a townhouse on the corner of Harvard and Bloomfield Avenues, a swank neighborhood of gated communities and exclusive shops. An expansive wall of windows offered a sweeping vista of the city. Three bedrooms, four bathrooms, a library, and an open floor plan provided ample space for entertaining. While Sam inspected the place, I tried to sit on one of the sleek black leather chairs in the living room but kept sliding off the slippery surface. I stood instead and waited in the foyer for him to finish. According to his agent, the home offered everything a bachelor like Mr. Seaforth might desire. I wasn't so sure.

"What do you think?" Sam asked after pacing the length of the living room for the third time. He stopped in front of the bar long enough to remove a peppermint from his pocket and popped it into his mouth.

"It's nice," I said, giving a polite smile to the realtor.

"But?" Sam leaned his back on the granite bar top and crossed his long legs at the ankles. Despite our differences and the years we'd spent apart, he could still read me and heard the reservation in my voice. "You don't like it."

"Well." I cast an apologetic glance at the realtor. She had brown, leathery skin, reminiscent of too many visits to the tanning bed. The corners of her mouth drooped at my next words. "It's not really your style, is it?"

"Why not? A fireplace in every room. A bar. What's not to like?" Sam frowned, too. He crossed his arms over his chest. I shook my head, not wanting to continue, but he pressed on. "Not big enough?" He turned to the woman. "Do you have anything else?"

"No. No." I rested a hand on his bicep and tried not to let the swell of hard muscle distract me. "This place is huge." I bit my lower lip, taking a beat to choose my words. "It's very nice."

I meant it. To my eyes, this penthouse seemed like a mansion. I'd grown up in a house trailer on the wrong side of town. My bedroom had been too small to accommodate more than a twin bed. The walls had been so paper thin, I could hear my brother fart in his sleep.

"You already said that. I asked for your opinion. You've never held back before. Don't start now," Sam said.

"Okay." My hesitation grew. He obviously liked the place, while my aversion continued to grow with each new room. Colorful modernist paintings hung on flat gray walls. Our footsteps echoed on the hard marble floors.

"Dakota." There it was. The way he said my name focused my thoughts. I turned in a slow circle and lifted my gaze to meet his. "Would you live here?"

"No."

"Why not? It's modern. Classy." He ran a hand over the gleaming black tile surrounding the fireplace.

"It's sparse and uncomfortable." We stared at each other. The Sam of my past liked the history and richness of antiques. "Too much granite and chrome."

"It will grow on you," he said. "You're just not used to this style."

"No. I won't. It's too cold," I said, shivering to underscore my statement, in spite of the warm sunshine outside the windows.

"Like me?" Tension thickened the air between us. His jaw clenched as he waited for my answer.

"I never said that. Don't put words in my mouth." I exhaled and tried to stay calm. "It's just not for me."

Sensing her tenuous hold on the sale, the lady chimed, "Of course, the colors can be changed to something warmer." Animosity brightened her eyes as she regarded me. They held nothing but sugary sweetness when they addressed Sam. "Or if you're interested in a total remodel, I know a decorator who would be happy to lend you a hand."

"No." Sam placed a hand on the small of my back and ushered us toward the front door, leaving the woman agape in the living room. The tension in his arm radiated up my spine. "Find something else."

We didn't speak again until we reached the car. Sam had always been reserved, the antithesis of my chattiness, but this silence harbored a new intensity. The stiffness of his shoulders and jaw encouraged my reticence. Miles of road flashed by outside the car. Buildings and sidewalks and lawns bathed in the early afternoon sunshine. I concentrated on the people living their lives, watched as they paused to stare at Sam's sports car, and wondered where they were going. After ten minutes, the vacuum of quiet became too much to bear. I felt the telltale internal heat of my temper rising.

"If you didn't want my opinion, you shouldn't have asked for it," I said in the quietest voice I could muster.

"You're damned frustrating," he growled.

"I don't know why you're pissed off. It's just an apartment."

"Townhouse," he corrected. His fingers drummed a rapid beat on the steering wheel. "And who says I'm pissed?"

"Why do you even care what I think? It's not like I'm going to be living there," I said before I realized the implication of the statement. It sounded like I hoped someday I might live there when I knew damn good and well our relationship was on precarious ground. We hadn't even been on a date. Even worse, it might suggest that I didn't want to ever live with him again when maybe I did. Had I just shut the door of opportunity? I turned to the window and wrinkled my nose, chastising myself for the slip. "What do I know?"

"Exactly." He downshifted, missed the gear, and cursed.

"You're the one who's frustrating." A tiny spark ignited my temper again. My mouth commandeered my brain and rallied for a siege of my common sense. "I still don't know why the hell I'm even here. Or did you just want me around so you could keep an eye on me? Make sure I'm not colluding with your father?" I huffed and crossed my arms over my chest, turning my torso toward the door. "Keep your friends close and your enemies closer."

"Do I need to worry?" The engine roared when he stepped on the gas to pass a slow-moving sedan.

"You're such a dick sometimes," I mumbled.

"What did you call me?"

"You heard me." I gasped and clutched the dashboard with both hands as he swerved the car to the curb.

He yanked the parking brake, jerking the car to a stop, and turned to face me. One of his hands fisted in the hair at my nape, pulling my face around to his. I stared at him, jaw clenched, daring him to say one more asinine thing. His nostrils flared and his gaze dipped to my mouth. Before I could draw breath, his lips were on mine, crushing and bruising in their need. I pushed at his chest with both hands. My arms softened when his tongue breached the barrier of my teeth.

A little whimper escaped me and wavered on the air between us. The tightness of his fingers relaxed in my hair. He growled, deep in his throat, the noise vibrating in his chest. The sweetness of his peppermint candy excited my taste buds and cooled my anger. When he pulled back at long last, my lips were wet and swollen, my mind completely blank.

"What was that for?" I asked, brushing the hair from my eyes with a shaky hand, and tried to fake some semblance of control.

"Just shutting you up for a minute." Smug satisfaction drifted across his expression. "You talk too much."

Chapter 5

Dakota

THE REST OF the day went by in a blur. We met to go over the information about MacGruder, but Sam said little outside of the context of business. When we were finished, he had Rockwell take me home but didn't emerge from his office to say goodbye. The snub rocked my fragile self-confidence.

When he called me to his office the next morning, I braced for the worst. Maybe he had changed his mind. Maybe he didn't want to try anymore. Maybe this attempt at reconciliation was nothing more than a charade meant to keep me close while he worked out the issues with his father.

I stood in front of his desk, hands fisted at my sides. He shuffled through a pile of papers, a scowl on his handsome face. When he didn't acknowledge my presence after a full minute, I coughed. "You rang?" I was unable to hide the sarcasm in my voice.

"Do you have a dress?" he asked, eyes still trained on his desk.

"I know you haven't noticed, but I'm wearing one right now," I said and tried to hide a smile of amusement at his exasperation.

Sam's gaze swept over my figure from head to toe, so long and with such intense scrutiny, my nipples pebbled beneath the silk of my dress.

"I meant a formal dress, smart ass." He bit his lower lip, and I knew he was trying to keep from smiling. After a beat, he blinked up to meet my gaze, green eyes twinkling.

"Um, no." I paused to run through a mental catalog of the contents in my closet. "I've got a couple of cocktail dresses. Why? Are you upscaling the dress code?"

"The Vandalia Charity Auction is next weekend. You're coming with me." He pushed his chair away from the desk and leaned back so far I thought he might tip. He pulled his wallet from the top drawer of his desk, withdrew a black credit card, and extended it toward me. "Here. Get what you need."

"Maybe I have plans," I said, feeling the need to be contrary. Just because I was in love with him didn't mean he could walk over me. The constant strain of having to prove myself was beginning to wear down my placidity.

"Like what?" He steepled his fingers in front of him and waited patiently for my answer.

"Plans. Things. Stuff." I waved a hand vaguely through the air. I wanted to visit my brother Crockett. Since our last interaction hadn't gone so well, I'd been avoiding a trip to the jail, but he was never far from my thoughts.

"Take it." Sam twirled the credit card between his fingers.

I frowned at the card and took a step back. "I'm not taking your money. I'll find something on my own."

"Take the damn card, Dakota." When his eyebrow lifted, I knew his patience was wearing thin. I crossed my arms over my chest and mirrored his expression. "Why can't you ever just do what I ask?"

"Because you don't ask. You order." I elevated my chin. "What happened to your manners? You used to be so polite."

His palm rasped over the stubble on his face. He blew out a breath, stood, and walked around the desk. I stared up at him, conscious of the heat from his body, the scent of his cologne, and the way he towered over me. When he hooked a finger in my belt and tugged me forward, my heart rate tripled. He brushed the back of his fingers over the line of my jaw.

"Dakota, please take the card." The soft whisper of his request caressed my ears. His touch caressed the soft skin of my neck. Desire shimmered through me. My resolve began to weaken. "It's a business event, and there are going to be a lot of important people there. I've invited John MacGruder and want you to help entertain him. I need you to look stunning." He smiled, putting all of his considerable charm into the request. "Please?"

"Well, if you insist." I took the card, but it felt uncomfortable in my hand. I stared at it, thinking of all the things it represented. Sam needed to know I wasn't interested in his wealth. If I spent his money, I'd be undermining my cause, his trust, and any chance at a future together. If I didn't take it, I'd be relegated to wearing a secondhand castoff from the local thrift shop. After weighing my options, I set the card on the desk and shook my head. "I can't use this, Sam. I appreciate the offer. It's very generous of you, but I can't. I'm sure I've got something I can wear."

"Really?" He seemed genuinely confused by my refusal. He let go of my belt and sat back on the desk.

"Yes." We stared at each other. I shifted my weight from one foot to the other but held fast in my stance.

"Is this how it's going to be?" The fingers of his left hand scratched over his chin, a very delectable chin peppered with stubble.

"Yes." I waited, my insides quivering as he contemplated my declaration.

Seconds dragged by, unnerving me. "You may as well get used to it."

"Then we have a problem," he said, his voice deep and rough. My knees shook but I kept my head lifted.

"That's your problem. Not mine." I crossed my arms over my chest. "You can't always have your way." When a muscle ticked in his jaw, my stomach twittered, but I soldiered on, buoyed by my conviction. "Don't be a brat, Seaforth."

His eyes narrowed, and his nostrils flared. I held back an inappropriate nervous giggle, knowing I'd struck a nerve. When his fingertip tilted my chin, I thrilled at his touch.

"Listen up, Atwell. From time to time, I may want to buy you things. Coffee. Lunch. Lingerie." The depths of his eyes glowed. All the muscles south of my navel clenched in response. "And it's your duty to accept them with grace and dignity for what they are--gifts."

"I can't," I whispered, although every fiber of my being yearned to comply. "I don't want you to think I'm using you." I blinked back the sting of tears, overcome with an irrational need to cry. "Maybe later. But not now. You'll have to compromise with me on this."

"I don't compromise," he said in a steel-edged voice.

"Then you need to learn, or this isn't going to work." I watched his chest deflate with an exasperated sigh. He tugged his lower lip between his teeth, denting the full flesh. This was going to go one of two ways. Either he'd respect me for setting a boundary, or he'd be angry at my refusal.

"Stubborn girl." He bent and brushed soft lips over mine in the sweetest of kisses. My heart danced in my chest. "Fine. No card." He swept the card off the desk and tucked it back into his wallet. "But you'll go see my friend. She's got a dress shop on the upper west side. She'll loan you something for the evening." I started to open my mouth in protest, but he pressed his index finger to my lips. "Compromise, remember?"

I bit the tip of his finger, rewarded by his brilliant smile. "Okay. I can do that."

Chapter 6

Dakota

OVERCOME WITH EMOTIONAL and mental exhaustion after work, I fell onto the sofa. With a glass of wine in hand, I switched on the TV and prepared for a relaxing evening. Even though the day had been tiring, my head swam with visions of Sam at his desk, the way he smiled whenever I came into his office, and the brush of his lips when he kissed me in the elevator. Knowing he wanted me around was the biggest ego trip I'd experienced in a long time.

I'd just propped my feet on the ottoman and set the station to my favorite zombie series when my cell phone buzzed. It was Muriel. For a brief moment, I considered letting the call go to voice mail before guilt prevailed. I hadn't talked to her in weeks, since she'd been let go. We weren't best friends, but I'd come to enjoy her company during the years we'd worked together.

"Hey, how are you?" I asked by way of greeting.

"I heard the horrible news about Harmony," she said, the frown evident in her voice. "Are you going to be okay?"

"What news?" I sat up and switched off the TV. I'd forced all thoughts of Harmony out of my head, finding them too painful. "I quit a couple of weeks ago."

"Seriously? Why didn't you tell me?"

"I'm telling you now." I rubbed the space between my brows with two fingers, easing the tension. I had no idea how to explain the convoluted situation with Sam and had avoided her for that very reason. Luckily, she was distracted by my next question. "So what happened?"

"Seaforth closed it down. He let everyone go but a handful of people. They shut the doors this morning. Brian said that bitch-troll Dahlia came in with severance checks for everyone and sent them home. Not Brian, of course. He's still there."

Nausea roiled my stomach. I thought of all the hard work Ansel had put into building the company, the way he'd treated his employees like family, and how sad he would feel to know it had all been for nothing. My next thoughts were of Valerie and her disabled husband, Melody with her two toddlers, and the other coworkers who needed their paychecks. My final thoughts were of Samuel Seaforth, his realtor, and their hunt for the perfect abode, spending the spoils of his acquisition. Flames of anger tinged my vision with red.

"I can't believe it," I growled through clenched teeth. "He said he'd be fair." I closed my eyes and counted to ten beneath my breath while Muriel carried on, oblivious. Conflicting emotions raced through my head. He'd promised to take care of everyone, and I'd believed him. I didn't know whether to feel betrayed or foolish.

"I guess it all depends on your definition of fair," Muriel countered. "I have to admit, he gave me a good severance package. I have an interview with his office for a marketing assistant position on Friday, but I'm going to cancel it. I don't think I can work for a man like that." She paused for a quick breath before continuing.

"What about you? Have you found anything else yet?"

I guess she wasn't as easily distracted as I'd hoped. "Well, I'm working for Sam--Mr. Seaforth--as a consultant. On a temporary basis," I rushed the confession and braced for her disapproval.

"Are you kidding me? I thought you hated him." Her voice raised an octave above normal.

"I don't hate him." It was true, but what I felt at the moment was much more complicated. Anger, resentment, and hurt jumbled together in a conflicted mishmash. This morning, I'd been overcome with excitement at the prospect of a new beginning with Sam. My hopes plummeted as I tried to reconcile the Sam I knew with the hard-nosed CEO of Infinity Enterprises. Was I so blinded by love that I'd misjudged him? I groaned and dropped my face into my hand in a weak attempt to hide from the reality of how little I really knew him.

"He's the enemy, Dakota. Men like Samuel Seaforth think money is more important than people. They profit from the misfortunes of others. All they care about is gobbling up anything and everything in their sight." She huffed. "Don't tell me you condone what he's done?"

"No. I don't." In truth, the longer I debated, the more furious I became. First thing tomorrow, I'd demand a full explanation. I had to believe there was a reason behind his behavior, something beyond monetary gain. I just couldn't accept that he'd commit such a duplicitous act, or that I'd misjudged him so horribly. "I think it's awful."

"Are you going to quit?" she asked. As if it was that simple.

"Quitting isn't going to accomplish anything." After a month of unemployment, my bank account had drained to the last penny. My mother's medical bills were mounting by the day, and she depended on me to help her with living expenses. "Except send me into bankruptcy." The intricacy of the situation cramped my brain. I massaged my left temple to ease the strain. "But I'm not sure how I can stay under the circumstances."

"What is this hold he has on you? I don't get it."

"It's complicated." I fought the need to explain myself. She wouldn't understand the depth of emotion and heartache tangled between Sam and me. If I didn't tell her, I would only be perpetuating the web of lies binding my past. The confession stumbled from my lips. "I got married. Right out of high school. We got divorced two years later. It was Sam."

"What?" Her laughter abraded my eardrum. I held the phone at arm's length. When I remained silent, her amusement halted. "Really?"

"Yes. Really." Anxiety rippled through me.

"You're not kidding?"

"No." The phone went silent.

"Oh, Dakota." Muriel drew in an audible breath while I braced for an explosion of questions that never came. "Separated for all these years and then *bam*, he shows up at your office. Now I understand the way he was always staring at you when you weren't looking and the way he chased you down in the lunchroom that day. That's so romantic. I mean, he's still a jerk, but wow. Just wow."

"It's not like that." Her unexpected revelation caught me off guard. I wanted to protest but couldn't find the right words.

"I need to know everything. How you met. Where you were married." She paused for breath, and I stole the opportunity to regain control of the conversation.

"I'll tell you all about it, but not right now. Okay?"

"Okay." By the quiver in her voice, I knew she wouldn't forget. "What are you going to do?"

"I don't know." My feelings clanged against each other. I wanted to believe in him. The part of me that loved him continued to think up excuses for his behavior, while the sensible side raged. I didn't hate him, but he wasn't winning any points by destroying everything I'd helped build. Even worse, he'd broken his promise to me. "I'll talk to him about it tomorrow," I said firmly. "I'd like to hear his side of the story. Maybe there's a reason."

This seemed to satisfy her for the interim, and I relaxed while she chatted about the new flavor of coffee at Joe's Java Junction and the cute guy moving in next door to her apartment. I had a difficult time following the conversation, however. My thoughts kept bouncing back to Sam and my displaced coworkers.

"And I think I'm going to ask him to the charity auction next weekend," she said. "Are you going?"

The auction. I'd forgotten about it. Sam had said I needed a dress. Anxiety began to build within me once more. Under the circumstances, I wasn't too keen on spending the workday with him, let alone a societal event where all eyes would be on us. "I'm not sure. Maybe."

Before I went anywhere with Sam, I needed an explanation for his actions. My optimistic side wanted to believe everything would work out, but the realistic side steeled for disappointment. And then what? Was I prepared to walk away from him when I'd only just found him? I sighed, took the glass of wine from its resting place on the coffee table, and chugged it down. I glanced at the half-empty wine bottle on the kitchen counter. After Muriel's phone call, one bottle wasn't going to be nearly enough.

Chapter 7

Sam

THE NEXT DAY, Dakota was waiting at the door when Rockwell pulled the car to the curb, and damn if she wasn't wearing the sexiest dress I'd ever seen. It was tight at the waist, the hem swirling around her thighs. The color matched the aquamarine hue of her eyes, setting my pulse into an uneven rhythm. I swore she wore stuff like that just to fuck with me. I stuttered in my phone conversation, eager to end the call and see how she was doing this morning. She greeted Rockwell with a bright smile as he opened the door for her. Warmth washed over me, the way it always did in her presence.

"My pleasure, miss," Rockwell replied, touching his hat before shutting the door behind her.

She slid into the seat next to me, hugging the door, eyes trained on the scenery outside. My warmth cooled. So did her smile. I lost track of the conversation with Mr. Takashima and had to ask him to repeat his question a second time.

"Good morning," I said and touched her hand once I'd ended the call.

She pulled away, curling her fingers in her lap. "Hey," she replied.

The icy greeting hit me like a punch to the gut. Under normal circumstances, rejection rolled off my back, but with her--it hurt more than I cared to admit. Since I'd been old enough to grow facial hair, I'd had women throwing themselves at me, but not Dakota. She'd divorced me and left me without a backward glance. A guy didn't come back from something like that without a few scars. I couldn't help reliving the pain every time she withdrew from me. I was holding my breath, waiting for her to leave again.

"Care to talk about it?" I asked, leaning into the opposite corner of the seat.

"No," she replied.

Dakota had never been a morning person, and I tried to dismiss her pique on this tidbit of knowledge. I'd always been the early riser in our relationship. When we'd been married, I used to tempt her from bed with pancakes and coffee. Sometimes we ate breakfast there, with her naked beneath the sheets. I would feed her bites from my plate, taking care to accidentally spill syrup on one of her breasts, looking for an excuse to lick it off. The memory caused a distinct, pleasant tightening in my groin. The furrow of her brows chased it away. I recognized that frown, and it usually meant I'd fucked up.

My male pride bristled. I hated the way she made me doubt myself. We'd been together less than three years, divorced for ten, yet one reproachful look had my guts in a knot. I sniffed, straightened, and glowered at the incoming call on my phone. Dahlia. Dakota saw it too. Her eyes narrowed, and she turned away again. I sent the call to voice mail and nudged her with my knee.

"What have I done now?" I asked, my voice harsher than I intended.

She faced me and cocked an eyebrow. "You tell me." Her eyes bored into mine, unrelenting, and hell if it didn't turn me on. Few men had the balls to glare at me the way she did, let alone call me out. "Why do you ask? Guilty conscience?"

"No." I dropped my gaze to the phone in my hand and pretended to scroll through the texts while I searched my brain for a clue as to what I'd done. Nothing came to mind. Frustrated, I tucked the phone into my pocket and scowled.

"Sam." Her disapproving tone set my teeth on edge. She sighed, clearly unhappy with me. "Did you forget to tell me something?"

I shook my head, still at a loss. "I'm not a freaking mind reader. You'll have to give me a hint."

She rolled her eyes. "Harmony?"

I studied her, recognized the simmering fury in her eyes, and flushed. Oh, yeah. Right. Overwhelmed with MacGruder, Takashima, and the search for an apartment, I might have forgotten to mention that. I felt the same way I had when I was ten and had broken a window with a baseball--defensive and guilty. "The doors are closed. You knew it was coming. I don't see the issue."

"You were supposed to absorb it, integrate it into Infinity. Hence the term *merger*." The cold flat tone of her voice chilled me. I'd never heard her speak that way to anyone, especially not me. "It means *to blend*, in case you didn't know."

"I know what it means."

We glared at each other. I was in the wrong, but I couldn't bring myself to admit it.

"You said you'd take care of everyone. That you'd make a place for them elsewhere." She met my eyes, nostrils flared, prepared for a fight.

"I did." My voice loudened in direct proportion to my growing irritation.

"No. You didn't," she snapped. "You took five people and let the other ninety-five go. I'd hardly call that *taking care of people*." She placed air quotes around the last four words with her fingers.

"So what should I have done? Give them all houses and new cars?"

By this time, we'd arrived at work. Dakota didn't wait for Rockwell to come around the car. She flung the door open before he reached the passenger side.

"You're a heartless bastard." She tossed the insult over her shoulder as she climbed out of the car and sprinted toward the entrance. "And a liar."

"Am not." I growled and grabbed my briefcase, squelching the urge to trot after her, too arrogant to admit she might have a point. She was up the stairs and into the office area within seconds. The girl had a set of legs on her. Mine were longer. I caught up to her quickly. "It's business, Dakota."

"Dirty business," she said, doubling her speed. The other employees were just getting coffee, settling into their desks and making idle chit chat before getting to business.

"Don't you walk away from me," I said, more loudly than appropriate for the workplace. "We're not done here."

Her office door slammed in my face. I jerked back just in time to save my nose from being smashed by the brass nameplate. The weight of a dozen pairs of eyes burned into my back, but when I turned around, everyone seemed engrossed in the floor. I yanked the cuffs of my shirt beneath my suit jacket and rolled my head on my neck to loosen the stiffness, daring anyone to comment. Mrs. Cantrell stood in the aisle, eyebrows arched to her hairline.

"What are you looking at?" I snapped.

"Dahlia is in your office," she said, obviously flustered.

"Good."

Dahlia rose from the chair to greet me. One look at my agitated face, and the smile slid from her lips. I tossed my briefcase on the desk and strode to the window. I stole a moment to reflect on the peaceful garden below. The emerald grass was punctuated with bursts of purple and red flowers. It reminded me of my childhood and simpler days. My harried thoughts calmed.

"Rough morning?" Dahlia asked.

"How many people did you hire from Harmony?" I turned to face her.

Although Dakota had told me, I wanted to hear it from Dahlia's lips. A small part of me still questioned Dakota's honesty. I hated myself for doubting her, but I was desperate to prove my innocence.

She shrugged. "A few. Only the ones worth having."

"How many?" I asked again, narrowing my eyes at having to repeat myself.

"Five or six."

"You were supposed to integrate them into the other offices," I said before sinking into my chair. "What part of that didn't you understand?"

"You said to choose the best and separate the rest," she answered, her tone cool. After seven years together, she'd grown used to my bluntness. "That's what I did. What I always do."

"You know that's not what I meant." I opened the top drawer of my desk and rummaged for an ink pen.

"That's exactly what you meant."

"Fuck," I grumbled under my breath and slammed the drawer shut. There was nothing I hated more than being in the wrong--which I clearly was.

"You said you trusted my judgment, to do whatever needed to be done." She lifted her face higher and crossed her arms over her chest. "It's done. Over. We discussed this. It's no different than any of the other companies we acquired." Her slanted brows drew together over her nose. "I appreciate your concern, but this is business, Sam. You pay me to make the hard decisions, and I did."

I pressed the intercom button. "Xavier. Get me some goddam pens, would you? You'd think a company this size would have pens."

He murmured in compliance while I focused all of my anger on the shortage of writing utensils.

Dahlia sighed and waited patiently for my annoyance to dissolve. "I don't understand why you're so upset," she said at last.

"I'm not upset," I replied through gritted teeth. "I'm just not sure how this miscommunication happened."

"It happened because you made it happen." The color of her complexion darkened to a deep rose red. She opened her mouth to say more, but Xavier entered. His gaze shifted between us, assessing the situation at once, and he wisely decided to stay silent.

"Thank you." I took the pens and shoved them into my drawer, having forgotten what I needed them for.

"Anything else?" Dahlia asked once Xavier had left.

"No. We're done."

"Next time, I'll be sure to get your okay on anyone who's cut loose," she said, jaw tight, and stood to leave.

I let her get all the way to the door before I spoke. "There won't be a next time."

She left my office in a snit, muttering to herself. A vague sense of unease remained with me. I hadn't climbed my way to the top by being a nice guy. As I went back to work, the image of Dakota's disapproving face remained in my thoughts. I didn't trust her, but maybe I was the one undeserving of trust. For the first time in my career, I had to wonder if I'd chosen the wrong path in life, if maybe I'd lost my humanity in the pursuit of revenge and retribution.

Chapter 8

Dakota

NO MATTER HOW hard I tried, I couldn't focus on price per square foot or the opportunity costs of any particular acquisition. The numbers shimmered on the computer monitor in a hazy blur, and it was all Sam's fault. He had absolutely no remorse about dismantling Harmony. In fact, he seemed proud of it. I didn't know that guy, the one who took pleasure in destruction, who profited from the ruination of others. My Sam had been sweet and thoughtful, kind and generous, and always concerned about the welfare of others. Where had he gone? I missed him, craved him, needed him.

After another unproductive minute, I surrendered to curiosity, opened the Internet browser, and typed in Sam's name. Millions of results popped onto the screen. Ten years of history flashed in front of my eyes. I sat back in my chair to process everything in front of me. I'd never been one to engage in social media, unwilling to risk seeing the Seaforth name or reopening the wound in my heart.

I scanned the topics. Mergers, acquisitions, and charity events filled the first page, snippets of information overloading my brain. *Samuel Seaforth is a tiger,* began one blog and went on to detail his systematic and ruthless dismantling of business after business. *Seaforth takes no prisoners,* warned another. I skimmed article after article about his rise to prominence.

An uncomfortable tightness gripped my chest. According to a piece from one of the business journals, Sam had amassed a respectable fortune through intelligent investment of his trust fund and an inheritance from his mother, but he stood to inherit billions from his father. I clutched the mouse until my fingers ached, scrolling through the items, hating what I saw but unable to look away. I had no idea his mother had passed. We hadn't been close. She'd never liked me, but I felt a pang of sadness for a life cut short. Samuel had adored her. He must miss her terribly. I thought about my own mother, how much I loved her, and was overcome with the urge to hug her.

Just as my anger began to dissipate, a new kind of distress swelled to a replace it. Pictures of Sam with other women, pretty women, sophisticated women. Each photo stabbed my heart like an ice pick. I wasn't naïve enough to believe there weren't other females in his life. Knowing it and seeing pictures of it were two different things. I might have been able to move past it, but it was the recurring photograph of one woman in particular that turned my blue eyes green with jealousy.

Tall, shapely, and stunning, her dark red hair flowed in loose, shining waves over her shoulders. In all of the photos, Samuel had an arm around her waist, and she had her hand on his chest, staring up at him with adoring eyes. A repressed profanity scratched my throat. I clicked on a random picture, intent on finding her identity, but before I could continue, Sam opened the door of my office and walked in.

"You and I need to get a few things straight," he announced without preamble.

"Can I get a lock on my door?" I scrambled to minimize the screen, sending a flurry of papers to the floor in the process. "Because apparently you have no regard for the privacy of others." I bent to retrieve the scattered pages, muttering beneath my breath. When I looked up, I found my eyes on the same level as the fly of his light gray trousers and the bulge behind it. I swallowed and straightened in the chair, lifting my gaze to meet his.

"You have to respect my decisions, Dakota," he continued. His green eyes studied me with determination. "I know what I'm doing. This is business, not personal. I can't have you questioning my authority. Especially in front of the other employees."

I folded my hands on top of the desk, striving for some semblance of control over my bouncing emotions. "You looked me in the eye and gave me your word that everyone would be treated fairly. The Samuel I knew always kept his promises. He cared about people."

"I never made any promises."

"You did."

"I didn't." He perched on the edge of the desk, his knee grazing my thigh. Attraction sputtered and sparked between us, at war with my anger. I was always so physically aware of his proximity, the way my body reacted to his. It was damn distracting. I vowed not to let it get the better of me.

"I've spoken with Dahlia. She assures me they were all given severance pay in line with their years of service. No one was left high and dry." He brushed his leg against mine. The deliberate contact tightened my nipples and everything south of my waist. "It's unfortunate we couldn't find a place for everyone."

I wrinkled my nose and pushed away from him. This wasn't the time to lose my head, no matter how strong the desire. A nuance of his cologne, subtle and masculine, hung in the air between us. "You're right. It's not my business. And it was unprofessional to close the door in your face." I could tell by the pulse of muscle in his jaw that he wasn't appeased by my confession, or the clipped tone in which it was delivered.

"And?" He lifted an eyebrow, waiting for an apology I had no intention of offering.

"And I'm not sure I know who you are anymore. I don't like what you did," I said, gaze flickering to the computer monitor and the hidden picture of him with the redheaded hottie. "You might be successful and rich, but you profit from the misfortunes of others. You used to hate people like that."

"We were kids then." His Adam's apple bobbed in his throat. "I didn't understand the way life works. It's messy and unpredictable, and only the strong survive." He put his hand over mine. I pulled it away. "You, of all people, should understand. You taught me that."

This statement stung in several unexpected ways. He still saw me as an opportunist, someone who valued winning over the rules of the game. Why wouldn't he? I'd chosen money over love. I'd betrayed him for financial gain. Never mind the blackmail or Crockett or my mother. In that moment, I felt more than defeated. I felt crushed.

"We're not the same. I never wanted to hurt anyone." I stared at my hands, clasped in my lap.

"But you did hurt me," he said in a cracked, husky voice. "You broke me, Dakota."

"I wanted to make things better." Tears pricked my eyes. I fought them away through sheer stubbornness. "I thought I was giving you back your future, not taking away your humanity."

"It's always going to come back to this, isn't it?" The pain in his voice struck a note inside me. These little hints at his vulnerability kept me coming back to him, time and time again, in spite of the ways he'd changed, the ways he was different. "We're never going to get past it."

We fell silent for a few seconds. I re-evaluated the events of the morning and our past. For a heartbeat, I wondered if he was worth the fight, if I'd made a huge mistake in accepting this temporary job, if the rift between us was too large to repair. One look into his face, and I knew he was thinking the exact same thing. He blinked away, as if embarrassed by the breach of his internal thoughts.

"I know we were married, but are we crazy?" I asked, my voice strained around the thickness of my throat. "To try this?"

He didn't answer right away. My heart banged against my chest while my head rallied for devastation. I didn't prepare for what happened next. He brushed the hair back from my forehead, his touch sweet and gentle. "Absolute freaking lunatics," he said, smiling, a dimple popping in his cheek. Tension I hadn't known existed drained from my body. His fingers traced around my cheekbone and down my jawline. "You've always made me crazy. I expect you always will."

I smiled back at him through a haze of tears and optimism. This was going to be so much more difficult than I'd ever imagined. Chances were good this venture would be a failure, but I had to know for sure. If I didn't try, I'd spend the rest of my life wondering.

"I think you were right. We need time to get reacquainted," I said. "We're both different people now." The Sam I'd married, the boy I'd loved, was a person of the past. This new Sam, arrogant and stubborn, was a stranger to me. Maybe I couldn't love this new man the way I'd loved the old one. Sadness filled all the cracks in my broken heart. Maybe I would have to let him go again. I wasn't sure I could withstand it the second time, but I needed to prepare for the possibility that we wouldn't make it.

"Yes." He stood, but not before a flicker of insecurity crossed his expression, as if he hadn't considered I might have my own suspicions and doubts. "We need time. *You* need time. I get it."

"Good." He needed to know I wasn't about to tumble headlong into a relationship with a man I no longer knew. He might have trust issues, but so did I. Even though the common thread of our past bound us together, our futures were headed in vastly opposite directions. No matter how much I'd loved him, I couldn't be with someone I didn't respect or trust.

I watched him walk to the door and tried not to focus on the width of his shoulders beneath gray linen, the narrowness of his hips, or the way his wavy blond hair brushed over the starched white collar of his dress shirt. When he reached the door, he turned. Our eyes met. The impact of our colliding gazes knocked the breath out of me. Sometimes he affected me that way, catching me unaware and unprepared for the strength of our attraction.

"Have you got a dress yet?" he asked, his voice low and gravelly.

The pit of my belly fluttered at the sound of it. One thing was certain, the physical attraction between us was just as strong as it had been our senior year in high school and every year of our marriage.

"No. I'm going tonight," I replied, nervous at the thought of the weekend together.

"Good." Silence stretched between us. "I thought maybe we could go to dinner tomorrow evening. Are you free?" he asked after a beat.

Was he asking me on a date? Perspiration dampened my palms. I pressed them together beneath the desk, desperate to appear calm. "I'll have to check my calendar and let you know," I replied. I needed time to think, and he needed to know I wasn't at his beck and call. A little rumination might do him good.

HIs mouth twisted in a reluctant grin. One lone dimple flashed in his cheek. "Okay. You do that. I'll be waiting." With a quiet thud, the door closed behind him.

I stifled a squeal of mingled excitement and trepidation. The man infuriated, frustrated, and confused the hell out of me, but I couldn't wait to see him again.

Chapter 9

Sam

I CARRIED DAKOTA'S wedding ring in my front pants pocket. It made me feel close to her even when we were apart. As I sat at my desk the next day, I withdrew the ring and slid it over the tip of my pinky. At thirty years of age, a man should know what he wanted. Beckett wanted security and happiness. Tucker wanted hot chicks and to attend the Burning Man Festival each summer. I'd thought I wanted to ruin my father and show him how badly he'd underestimated me, but revenge no longer satisfied the emptiness inside me. What did Dakota want? Two months into our reunion, I had no idea.

I'd seen the disappointment in her eyes over the situation with Harmony. It killed me to know I'd put it there. Before we'd divorced, I'd been her hero. I'd seen it in her smile and felt it in her touch. No one ever loved me the way she had. I wanted that feeling again. I wanted her to look at me the same way she had all those years ago.

"Are you ready to go over a few things?" Mark, head of accounting, stood in front of my desk, prepared for our meeting.

"Yes." Shaking thoughts of Dakota from my head, I put her ring back into my pocket.

We moved to the conference table. Mark spread out a dozen financial reports, graphs, and statements over the surface. For the next two hours, he pored over the figures with impressive thoroughness. With each passing minute, my gut tightened a little bit more. Mark's face was pale as he gathered up the papers and prepared to leave but not as pale as mine.

"Basically," he said, "you're broke."

Alone in my office, I tried to make sense of my thoughts. I'd been so busy wreaking havoc on the corporate world, so bent on destroying my father that I'd failed to protect my personal assets. Over the course of the last two years, I'd spent every dime I had on blocking Malcolm Seaforth's acquisitions. I kept thinking one more deal would be the turning point. I'd become a gambler, raising the stakes with every merger, borrowing money from one company to fund another in a desperate shell game.

Time was running out. If I wanted MacGruder, I needed to make a move soon or the window of opportunity would close. It was a risk I'd have to take. I didn't care if I lost everything I owned. I just wanted to hurt my dad the way he'd hurt me, so I went after the most precious thing in his life--his business. He had big money invested in the development of a new stadium outside St. Louis. I'd been systematically buying up all the surrounding properties, hedging him in. I planned to zone the properties and sit tight on them, creating costly delays and years' worth of planning commission issues. MacGruder held the final piece of the puzzle. I sensed victory, and old habits commandeered my thoughts. I wanted to win. I needed to win. It would cost me everything, but it was worth it.

"Mr. Seaforth? A courier just delivered a package for you," Xavier announced over the intercom.

"Take care of it," I snapped, too overwhelmed to be bothered with mundane things.

"It's marked personal and confidential," Xavier continued. "For your eyes only." My bluntness never bothered him, or if it did, he didn't show it. "You'll have to sign for it."

"Fine. Send him in." With a groan of exasperation, I turned my chair to face the door. A young man entered the room, an express envelope in one hand. I provided my electronic signature, and he handed the envelope to me. There was no return address, nothing to indicate what it was for or whom it came from. I ripped open the top and drew out a manila envelope with Dakota's name scrawled across the front in my father's handwriting. A note was attached to the outside.

A cold finger of dread snaked down my back. The man never gave up. I considered tossing the whole thing into the shredder but stopped myself. What if it was something intended to hurt her? The man had no boundaries when it came to playing with people's lives, mine included. I scanned the message and closed my eyes to process the intent behind such an act.

I thought you might like to see what your ex-wife has been up to in your absence. No need to thank me. Sincerely, Malcolm. It wasn't lost on me that he'd signed the note with his first name, as if I wouldn't know him otherwise.

I read the note again and again, searching for clues in the spaces between the words. What kind of father did something like this? My next instinct was to open the file and scour the information. I'd had a burning curiosity about where she'd been and what she'd done during our years apart. She'd been in my thoughts every day since I'd met her, even after our divorce. I turned the envelope over in my hands, undid the clasp, and ran a finger beneath the sealed seam.

I stopped short of withdrawing the documents. Malcolm wanted me to read this. The only reason he'd sent it was to hurt me or Dakota with whatever vitriol it contained. If I opened it, I'd be playing into his plans to derail my life. After a minute, I fastened the clasp and shoved the envelope to the back of my top desk drawer. I wanted to know everything about Dakota, but I wanted to learn it from her, in our own good time.

The right thing would've been to drop the entire package into the shredder, but I just couldn't bring myself to do it. In spite of all the horrible things he'd done, I wanted to trust my father. I wanted to believe he loved me and had my best interests at heart. He continued to insist Dakota was my Achilles heel. What if he was right, and I was just being stupid about her--again?

Chapter 10

Dakota

THE NEXT MORNING, Rockwell waited at the curb in front of my apartment. His sunny smile brightened the gray morning. I was disappointed to find the interior of the car empty. Sam's schedule for the day was slammed with back-to-back meetings, Rockwell explained.

Sam and I hadn't spoken since the previous day. He'd left work early to attend an off-site meeting. Rockwell had offered to take me home, but I'd taken the bus instead, needing the time to reflect. Although our conversation had ended on a positive note, the disparity of our opinions demonstrated just how different we had become. We were strangers who'd once been married. He was a predator and a destroyer, while I only wanted to help others build their dreams. He'd been that way too once, before his dad, before the divorce, before me. I wanted to believe that person still existed inside him somewhere. I refused to give up on us until I knew for certain there was no hope.

Rockwell dropped me in front of the office. The other employees were just arriving. Their gazes flicked to Sam's car, to Rockwell then to me, fitting all the puzzle pieces together. No one met my eyes as I walked inside and up the stairs. Without anyone saying a word, I knew what they were thinking, and it wasn't flattering. I got a cup of coffee and settled into my office, prepared to finish Sam's research, and tried to push it out of my mind. Let them gossip and speculate. I had business to take care of.

It was mid-morning when my interoffice messenger dinged. I flinched at the unexpected sound. Curious to see who might be contacting me, I clicked on the icon and smiled to find Sam's name.

Sam: Have you decided yet?

Me: About what?

Sam: About dinner.

Me: Yes

Sam: Yes you've decided or yes to dinner?

My fingers hovered over the keyboard. I decided to wait before responding, to build his anticipation. It wouldn't do to appear too eager, especially when he always seemed to have the upper hand. I gritted my teeth and let five minutes pass before typing out my reply.

Me: Yes to both

It was my turn to wait. He didn't reply for a full thirty minutes. I squelched the urge to bite my nails and returned my attention to work. Every ten seconds or so, I glanced at the messenger box until at last it dinged with his answer.

Sam: Stellar. So you aren't mad at me?

Me: That's still under debate.

Sam: Can we agree to disagree?

Me: Yes but I'm right and you know it.

Sam: LOL. Pick you up at 8. Don't be late. You know how I hate that.

Me: Don't be a dick. You know how I hate that.

The response had barely left my messenger when the phone rang. I stared at it. No one had called me since I'd started working there. In fact, no one had even shown me how to use the phone. After a few tense seconds, I found the pickup button and lifted the receiver.

"About damn time." Sam's deep voice sent a thrill straight between my legs.

"So impatient, Mr. Seaforth," I said, biting back a smile of delight, feeling an instant relief of tension over our disagreement.

"Do you really think your boss is a dick?" he asked, laughter lilting in his tone.

"I know he is." In spite of all my reservations about us, I dissolved into a simpering schoolgirl, twisting a lock of my hair around my finger as I spoke. "But I like him anyway."

"And why is that?" His tone became throatier, more intimate.

"Well, he's very hot."

"Is he?"

"Yes. He's got these fantastic green eyes," I said, throwing myself into the conversation with reckless abandon. "And he's got a very nice ass."

His chuckle vibrated through me. "Does he now? Is that important to you?"

"Oh, yeah. The ass could be a deal breaker." I bit my lower lip, waiting for his reply, wondering if I'd pushed the topic too far.

"Just so you know, I like your ass too." The humor in his voice buzzed through me, giving me a drug-like high.

"Good to know." I bit my lower lip, flushing with pleasure.

"Get back to work, Ms. Atwell," he said, and hung up the phone.

By the time Sam arrived at my apartment, I'd managed to work myself into an unprecedented frenzy. I still didn't know if this was or wasn't a date. A pile of unsatisfactory clothing sat in a heap on my bed. I'd changed outfits a dozen times before settling on a pair of dark blue jeans, a white blouse, and low-heeled sandals. With my hair pulled into a high ponytail, I looked younger than my thirty years, a glimmer of my teenage self, the girl he'd married.

I took one last look in the mirror before heading to answer the door, stomach churning with anticipation. The sight of him, tall and elegant at my threshold, reminded me of all the reasons I wanted things to work out between us. He swept a lingering look from my head to toes, smile fading.

"I'll go change," I said, flushing with embarrassment at the miscommunication. He wore a beautiful navy blue suit, pinstriped shirt, and red necktie. He was ready for a night at the country club, while I'd dressed for a hayride.

"No. You're fine," he said, extending a hand to touch my arm. The tiny hairs above my wrist prickled at the contact. "My fault."

"I assumed--I mean, you said I could pick the place. I thought we'd go for beer and pizza." I floundered, feeling one hundred different kinds of foolish. It had been our favorite type of evening when we'd been married. But we weren't married. Not anymore. We weren't even the same people. How silly to think I could resurrect the past.

"I came straight from work." As he spoke, he yanked on his tie and pulled the knot loose. He slipped out of his jacket and dropped it over his arm. "Better?"

I smiled, our gazes colliding. "Hang on a second." I stepped forward and placed a hand on his chest. His breath hitched at my touch. The warmth of his body heated my breasts as I stood on tiptoe to unbutton his collar. "There." His arm came around my waist to steady me. "Why do you wear these stuffy suits? You always hated them."

"If you want to be successful, you need to look successful," he said, smiling down at me. "Most people aren't intimidated by a guy in jeans and a T-shirt."

"Don't you ever relax? Get casual?"

We stared at each other. My gaze dipped to his lips.

"I'm relaxing now," he said. "I could go home and change if you like."

"No. It's fine." I held my breath, wishing he would kiss me and knowing he wouldn't. There were too many unsettled questions between us. We'd come a long way, but we had even further to go.

"Ready?" he asked. When I nodded, he threaded his fingers through mine. I held back the surprise I felt inside and let him lead me down the hallway to the elevator. Tiny tingles of pleasure climbed my arms and buoyed my hopes. Perhaps this was a date after all. Our hands stayed linked all the way to the sidewalk outside, his palm warm and strong against mine. The evening air was soft, redolent with the scent of newly awakened summer. I was surprised to find the Porsche waiting at the curb and not Rockwell.

"Where's Rockwell?" I asked.

"He asked for the night off." Sam released my hand to open the car door for me. "I think he has a girlfriend."

"Really?"

"Yeah, really," Sam said, sliding into the car next to me. "He got a haircut today and borrowed my cologne. I think he's hoping to get laid."

I snorted, appalled and amused by the thought of steadfast Rockwell trolling for sex. "I hope it's someone worthy of him." The dash lights illuminated the planes and angles of Sam's face. I placed a hand over my belly to calm the nervous twitter there. I had no idea how to act. I was hyper aware of his body, every move as he shifted through the gears, the sideways glances when I spoke.

We went to a nearby pizza joint, where the waitresses wore tight T-shirts and short skirts. It was a small, cozy establishment with large flat-screen TVs and dark, intimate booths. Sam ordered a pitcher of beer along with our pizza. It was comfortable, familiar, and surreal all at the same time.

"How did your meetings go today?" I asked to break the awkward silence.

"Fine." Beneath the table, his feet shifted until one of his knees rested between mine. The deliberate move caused a delicious clenching in my core. "I don't want to talk about work."

"Okay." The way he stared at me, eyes intense and dark, caused the blood to rush into my face. "What do you want to talk about?"

He leaned back against the booth bench. The collar of his shirt gaped open to reveal a smattering of gold hair against sun-bronzed skin. "I want to talk about you. I know who you were, but I want to know who you are now." His knee brushed against mine. Up. Down. Up again.

A rush of adrenalin exploded through my veins. I wasn't sure why I was so nervous. We'd been married. He'd seen me without makeup, when I was pallid from the flu, sick with food poisoning, and in various states of undress. He shouldn't affect me like this, but he did.

"I wouldn't know where to start." I bit my lip and blinked away, uncertain.

"How about from the beginning?" His hand found mine and squeezed.

I smiled at him, and he smiled back. With his hair ruffled and one arm thrown over the back of the bench, he looked like the carefree Sam of my memories. I began to think we might be able to work things out after all.

Chapter 11

Sam

AFTER WE ATE, we walked along the boulevard and toward the park. It was a quiet street, devoid of the smells and sounds of downtown. Crickets chirped. A dog barked from a distance. Laughter floated out the open doors of bistros and wine bars. An occasional couple strolled past us, nodded and smiled, as if we were one of them. It reminded me of our walks after high school, the awkward silences, the thrill of an accidental brush of our shoulders, wondering if she'd let me kiss her goodnight. In this one respect, not a lot had changed over the years. The similarities put our situation into perspective for me with unnerving clarity. We still had awkward silences. I still thrilled at our accidental touches. I still wanted to kiss her goodnight. And I was arrogant enough to hope that I might get lucky.

"I can't believe we haven't run into each other before," she said after another one of our quiet moments. "We know a lot of the same people."

"I opened the office here last year, but I've spent most of my time at the

Chicago office." I moved aside to allow a kid on rollerblades to pass us then fell into step beside her again. "I don't usually get involved in the operational side of takeovers." As soon as I said it, I knew I'd opened the lid on a topic better left untouched. "My job is to close the deal and move on to the next one."

"Why?" She stopped and turned to face me in front of the fountain. It was a huge, showy affair. Two mermaids perched in the center, seahorses surging outward from the perimeter. The sound of splashing water mingled with the plaintive refrain of a saxophone from a nearby jazz bar. "Too messy? Don't want to get your hands dirty?"

"No." I drew in a deep breath. I needed to choose my next statement carefully. "I have a limited amount of time. If I did everything, nothing would get done. That's why I hire people to handle those things."

"But you were knee deep in Harmony's acquisition." Stubborn girl. I knew she wouldn't stop digging until I provided a satisfactory answer.

"I might have had a personal interest in it."

We resumed walking. Our footsteps thudded softly on the pavement. I became acutely aware of her next to me, her head level with my shoulder, occasional hints of her perfume wafting among the scents of fresh-cut grass and flowers.

"You mean me."

"Yes." I was grateful for the darkness between yellow pools of streetlight so she wouldn't see the heat in my cheeks. "The second I saw your name on that employee roster, nothing could've kept me away."

"You hated me." The plaintive truth of her statement flattened my mood.

"I never hated you. Not exactly." While I groped for words, she stopped to stare at me, hands on hips. "Okay. Maybe a little," I admitted.

"And now?" The intense scrutiny of her blue-green eyes made me weak at the knees. How could I give her an answer to a question I kept asking myself over and over? A part of me wanted to hate her, to continue the charade and bask in the safety of animosity. But a bigger part couldn't stop thinking about her, the scent of her hair, the softness of her lips, the way her nose wrinkled when she was thinking. Reality hit me in the chest like a percussion blast.

"How can I hate you, Kota, when you were my first love?" *My only love.* As soon as I confessed, panic squeezed my lungs. Jesus, what was wrong with me? I'd very nearly professed my undying devotion to the woman who'd crushed my heart and my balls in one fell swoop. I tried to backpedal and save myself. "I mean, you'll always be special to me." I felt her stiffen from two feet away. "We had something special once." The more I spoke, the darker her expression became. "You were very special." My voice died away. I was fucking up. Big time.

"If you say *special* one more time, I will punch you in the nuts."

I laughed at the adorable scowl on her face. A light breeze lifted the hair over her forehead. Moonlight glowed on the curves of her lips and cheeks. She'd never been more beautiful or--I realized a split second too late--more pissed. The next thing I knew, she spun around and walked in the opposite direction at impressive speed.

"Wait. Where are you going?"

She flipped me the bird.

"Dakota, come on." I paced after her. "Seriously?"

I caught up to her in four strides, slipped an arm around her waist, and swung her around to face me. We stood facing each other, her soft body pressed to mine, held by the pressure of my arm. I could feel every inch of her. The rise and fall of her ribs with each breath. The pillowy softness of her breasts. The button fly of her jeans cutting into my groin. We lined up perfectly this way and always had.

"Dakota." I stared into her eyes, mesmerized by the tiny flecks of green and gold, narrowed with irritation and hurt. My lips brushed hers. She stiffened, but I didn't let go. She needed to know I meant business. Against her mouth, I whispered, "You're still special to me. I can't be in the same room with you and not want to touch you. I hold my breath waiting for one of your smiles." Delicate nostrils flared the tiniest bit, like a doe scenting the wind. "You were the best and worst part of my life. I'll never have with anyone else what I had with you. It's just not possible."

The rigidity of her spine relaxed a fraction. We were alone on the street, sheltered by the drooping limbs of a willow tree. A mass of flowers spilled from giant urns next to us in chaotic colors of purple, red, and yellow. Their sweet scents floated in the air around us.

"You talk like we're past tense. Like we're already over," she said.

I kissed her again, softly this time. Her lips melted against mine. Their sweetness tantalized me, persuading my tongue to seek hers. Sexual awareness hummed through my body as the kiss deepened. She felt good in my arms, and for a few blissful minutes I was able to forget her betrayal, the divorce, and everything in between.

"Baby," I murmured, "we're just getting started."

Chapter 12

Dakota

THE INSTANT SAM'S lips touched mine, I was done for. It had always been that way. I could no more control my body's response to him than I could the shifting of the wind. My nipples stiffened, my heartbeat tripled, and the space between my legs ached. In alternating measures, he frustrated and infuriated me, thrilled and terrified me. When his fingers spread over my back, pressing me to him, I dissolved into him.

"You don't fight fair," I said when he withdrew his mouth and leaned his forehead against mine.

"I do what it takes to win," he murmured. The vibrations of his voice rumbled through his chest and into mine.

"Are we in a battle?" I turned my face up to his and searched his eyes. They were dark and somber.

"Sure seems like it." His chuckle preceded the possessive tightening of his arms around my waist. "To the death."

"Why does it have to be so flipping hard?" I toyed with the buttons of his shirt, enjoying our closeness. I belonged in his arms. It was one of those moments where everything seemed to be as it should. The stars had aligned and brought me to him at this precise moment in time. Nothing had or ever would be so perfect again. "Do other people have to work this hard to be together? Because I'm telling you, this thing between us might kill me."

Laughter shook his chest. He pressed a kiss to my temple. "If we don't kill each other first."

Wind rustled through the tree limbs above us. The city bus stopped at the curb across the street, and a rowdy group of boys tumbled down the steps. "Get a room," they shouted amid hoots and whistles. We both laughed this time and broke apart to continue down the sidewalk.

We made our way back to my apartment. He kissed me on the steps outside the building. I clung to him, not wanting the night to end, and buried the fingers of my right hand in his thick hair. Every time he kissed me, it was like the first time. His tongue swept over mine in a playful dance, teasing and tantalizing. I leaned into him, wanting more, and was disappointed when he pulled back.

"Come upstairs," I whispered, gazing into his eyes, drunk on his presence and his touch.

"Not tonight." He shook his head. My tummy twittered at the rejection.

"Why not?" I pressed against him, enjoying the heat of his muscular torso against me, hoping to change his mind.

"As much as I want to make love to you, I think maybe we should both take a step back. It's been great tonight, and I want to end things on a good note."

"Is this a good note?" I asked and lifted on my tiptoes to meet his eyes, dragging my breasts along his chest in the process.

He groaned. "Now who's not playing fair?"

"I like to win, too." I tangled my fingers with his and tried to tug him up the steps. "Come on. I promise to make it worth your while."

He smiled and brushed a lock of hair back behind my ear with an index finger. "I've got an early meeting tomorrow morning, and I need to do some work tonight to prepare." When he stepped back, cool air rushed between us, chilling me. "Another time."

"Okay." I tried to hold back the frown looming on my lips. Confused, I dropped his hand. I thought things had gone well between us, but now I wasn't so sure. "Next time then."

He touched the tip of my nose with his finger. "That's a promise, sweet pea."

Chapter 13

Dakota

WHEN I WENT into Sam's office for our afternoon meeting the next day, lines of worry creased the corners of his eyes. My deep-seated insecurities began to resurface, and my confidence flagged. I'd seen that look during our marriage, when our checking account was overdrawn or after one of our fights. I bit my lower lip, anxiety overriding the pleasant, lingering aftertaste of our date the night before.

We went over the MacGruder information with excessive thoroughness. He hardly spoke to me, except to ask questions about the data, and when he did, his tone was brusque. The disparity between his work persona and his after-hours persona kept me off balance. I had no idea how to blend the two personalities or if I even should. With each passing minute, my unease grew until I squirmed in my seat.

After another hour of answering his rapid-fire interrogation, I placed a hand in the center of the report he was reading, forcing him to stop and look at me.

"What?" he asked. Most of the time his eyes were bright and alert, but today a vacant shadow clouded their depths. He tried to slide my hand out of the way. I resisted.

"Breathe, Sam," I admonished gently. He blinked, coming back to himself and subsequently back to me. "We've been at this for hours. Let's take a break."

"I need answers. Today." He pushed away from the table and paced to the window.

"What's the hurry? Our meeting with MacGruder isn't until next week." Although his stance blocked my view of his face, the tension in his shoulders broadened the top line of his suit. He shoved his hands into his pockets.

"I'm moving up the meeting."

"Why?" The note of urgency in his voice renewed my unease. "These kinds of things shouldn't be rushed. You know that."

"There you go, telling me how to run my business again." His voice held a note of quiet disapproval.

When he turned to face me, I curled my fingers into fists to curb the warring desires to either touch him or slap him. I wasn't certain how to handle this Sam. The midday sun poured through the window behind him, outlining the inverted triangle of his shoulders and hips, the length of his legs, and the wavy mess of his hair. He looked tough, overtly masculine, and unapproachable.

I stood and walked around the table, trailing my fingers over the surface, taking my time. He stared down at me, eyes hooded, until I came to a stop in front of him. I rested my rear end against the table, hands gripping the edge, and stared back.

"I don't doubt your ability to run your business," I said. "You've made quite a success of yourself without my help." I spread my knees, skirt drawn between them, one leg on each side of his. I hooked a finger into his belt, drawing him toward me with a gentle tug. "I'm just stating the obvious. MacGruder is a hard sell. You're forcing him to give up a lifetime of work. He's not going to roll over and die. He might act meek and resigned, but I guarantee you, he's not."

A muscle flexed below his cheekbone, a telltale sign of his growing consternation. "I know that."

"I know you know that." While I stared up into his eyes, I ran my hands from his knees to his hips, feeling the swell of thigh muscle and the indentation of his glutes beneath my palms. When I reached the waistband of his trousers, he exhaled. "So what's your hurry?"

"I have a schedule to follow and deadlines to meet in order to reach my goal." The lines around his eyes softened the tiniest bit. "Time is running out."

I traced the waist of his pants to his fly and unbuckled the belt, never letting my gaze leave his. "And what is your goal, Mr. Seaforth?"

"To find out what kind of panties you have on under that sweet little dress," he said, the hint of a smile tugging at his lips. He cupped my chin and rubbed his thumb over my lower lip. I bit it gently and was rewarded by the hiss of his breath.

"Didn't your mother ever tell you the story about the tortoise and the hare? Slow and steady wins the race, right?" I took his thumb into my mouth, sucked on the tip, swirling my tongue around it. His nostrils flared, sending a flutter of excitement into my belly. I let go of his thumb with a *pop*. The salt of his skin lingered on my tongue.

"Sometimes." Green eyes darkened to black as his pupils dilated. "Sometimes I like to come in hard and fast." He caressed my cheek. I turned my face and kissed his palm. A flicker of heat and desire crossed his expression before he dug his fingers into the hair at my nape and tugged my head back. The seemingly cruel gesture was laced with tenderness, erotic in its intensity. A thrill like no other weakened my knees.

"Is the door locked?" I asked.

"Yes."

The ragged need in his voice called to me. I kneeled in front of him. A muted growl broke the silence in the room as I unzipped his fly. I palmed the hard ridge behind his black boxers, the silken fabric smooth and heated. He pushed into my hand, growing longer and thicker with each passing second. I loved knowing I made him this way, that I could still turn him on after so many years apart.

"You pay all these people to answer to you, but I have to wonder...who do you answer to?" I slipped his pants over his hips, drawing his boxers down with them. His erection bobbed in front of me. "Who keeps you in check, Sam? Who looks out for you?" I placed a light kiss on the tip of his cock.

"No one." The husky admission pained my heart. Strong, relentless Sam had no one. Even I, his wife, had abandoned him. "I look out for myself."

By this time, I held his erection in my hand. I tickled the head of his cock with my tongue before taking him into my mouth. He moaned and tightened his fingers in my hair. The sound blanketed my soul, erased my doubts, and filled me with desire. Desire to take care of him, desire to cherish him, to be the one person he could always count on.

To demonstrate my point, I took him deeper in my mouth until he hit the back of my throat. Smooth skin slipped through my lips. His hips moved forward, overwhelmed by the instinctive urge to thrust. I fisted the base of his cock to control his movements, enjoying the power. When I glanced up, his head was thrown back, Adam's apple bobbing in his lean throat, eyes closed, and lips parted.

I'd only given him head a few times while we'd been married. It wasn't that I didn't like it. I'd just never felt very skilled in that area, and he'd never complained about the lack. I'd been a twenty-year-old girl then. A decade later, the number of items in my sexual bag of tricks had increased exponentially. To demonstrate, I flattened my tongue and dragged it along the thick, pulsing vein on the underside of his erection. I closed my eyes and reveled in the physical sensations of such an intimate act, undone by the spicy scent of his cologne, the heat of his skin, and the staccato grunts from his throat.

"Shit," he muttered. "If you keep doing that, I'm going to come in that smart mouth of yours."

I paused long enough to look up at him, my fist tight around him. "That's the point, isn't it?"

His tongue passed over his lower lip, and his fingers dug deeper in my hair, cupping the back of my head when I took him back into my mouth. I liked the feeling of tension between us, the way he tried and failed to control his emotions. One corner of his lips curled up in a boyish smile.

"So fucking sweet, Dakota. You looking up at me like this." He brushed his thumb over my cheek. "My girl."

My heart swelled until my ribs ached. I was his girl. I always had been. And he was my guy. My Sam. He owned me from the inside out. A need to possess him in the same way spurred my lips to action. I dragged my teeth over his length, lightly but with enough pressure to make him hiss with pleasure. I still didn't know where I stood with him, but at this very moment, it didn't really matter. We were Sam and Dakota, high school sweethearts, married, divorced, and still as hot for each other as the day we'd met. To prove my point, I massaged his head with the texture of my tongue, smooth against rough, and felt him jerk as the last vestiges of his control dissipated. Ten seconds later, he came with a ragged growl and both hands fisted in my hair.

"Mr. Seaforth, your conference call starts in five minutes. I have them holding on line two." Mrs. Caldwell's disembodied voice floated from the intercom on the table, causing me to flinch in surprise.

"We're just about done here," he said, his control impressive. I smirked and flicked my tongue over his fading hardness, earning a playful glare. "Thank you, Mrs. Cantrell."

His hands shook as he disentangled his fingers from my hair. He smoothed his palm over the side of my face, smiling down at me. With his large hands on my biceps, he urged me to my feet. We walked the four steps to his private bathroom. I sat on the sink while he used a washcloth to wipe my face. The tender gesture broke down the last of my defenses. If I'd had any doubts before, I knew with certainty now. Somewhere inside this complicated man existed the love of my life. He was still there, and he still loved me. He just hadn't realized it yet.

Chapter 14

Dakota

THE FOLLOWING MONDAY, it was well past midnight when my doorbell rang. I ignored it. Although I was exhausted, I'd been drifting in and out of sleep for the past hour. When banging replaced the doorbell, I cracked one eye and sat up. If whoever it was kept up their ruckus, the neighbors would certainly call the cops.

"Hold your horses," I grumbled. "I'm coming. I'm coming." As I stumbled toward the door, I pulled on an oversized T-shirt.

I lifted on tiptoe to peer through the peephole. Crockett stood outside my door, hands shoved in his pockets, a frown on his face. The last I knew, he was still in jail, awaiting trial. I'd never expected to find him at my doorstep in the middle of the night.

I opened the door. He brushed past me into the kitchen, pulled a carton of milk from the refrigerator, and drank out of the open top. "Thank fuck you're home," he said. "My key doesn't work."

"I changed the locks," I said. His appearance unsettled me for a number of reasons. Chiefly because dealing with him required an enormous amount of self-control and mental effort. "What are you doing here?" I remained at the foyer, front door gaping open.

"Good to see you, too, sis." He peered over the top of the milk at me then shrugged. "I got released."

"No shit, Einstein. How?" Recovering, I shut the door and crossed my arms over my chest.

"Don't you worry about it. God, I'm starving." After a quick perusal of the fridge, he grabbed a carton of leftover Chinese and began to pick out pieces of General Tsao's chicken with his fingers. "Jail food is crap."

"When did you get out?"

"Yesterday." He carried the food to the sofa, where he collapsed onto the cushions with a heavy sigh.

"You can't stay here."

"Oh, come on, Kota. Just for tonight." With a contented growl, he propped his feet on the coffee table and pointed the remote at the TV. "I spent last night on the street. You have no idea how weird that was. Did you know there's, like, an entire homeless community living under the expressway bridge?"

The idea of my baby brother sleeping under an interstate highway like some kind of hobo brought the sting of tears to the backs of my eyes. My resolve wavered and crumbled. I couldn't turn him away, could I? My mother always preached forgiveness. How was I any better than Crockett? I wanted Sam to forgive me. Wasn't I being a hypocrite--withholding forgiveness to one person while seeking it from another?

"Fine. One night." I rubbed my eyes, too tired to continue the fight. "Tomorrow you have to find somewhere else to stay."

"Sure. Thanks," he replied through a mouthful of food. "You got any ice cream?"

Back in my bed, it occurred to me that we had come full circle. Crockett was back under my roof. I was once again pining for Sam. How did this keep happening? The bedcovers rustled with each of my movements as I sought for a comfortable position and found none. Ten years had passed, and yet nothing had changed.

When morning arrived, I woke Crockett with a shake of his shoulder. He scowled and rolled away. I shook him a second time with more force. Sam and Rockwell would be arriving any minute, and I needed Crockett out of the apartment before I left.

"Get up." I yanked the covers away and tossed them onto a chair. "I have to leave for work."

"Dakota," he whined. "Come on. I'm exhausted." I opened the curtains. Bright yellow sunshine puddled on his face. He threw a forearm over his eyes. "I'll lock up when I leave."

"No, Crockett." When he didn't budge, I pulled the pillow from beneath his head and bopped him in the face with it. "You can't stay here. I'm serious."

"Fuck." He sat up, rubbing his eyes, hair limp over his forehead. "Fine. I don't know where you expect me to go at this ungodly hour."

"How about to the Urban Employment Office?" I picked up his shoes from the floor and tossed them at him. "They have these things there called jobs. Maybe you could get one."

"I've already been down there. They don't have anything."

"Then go back and ask again. And tomorrow and the day after." I shouldered the strap of my purse and nudged him toward the door. "You can come back when you have a job."

Once he saw the determination on my face, he sighed and trudged down the hall to the elevator with me. We rode downstairs in silence. At the front door, he caught sight of Sam standing next to the car chatting with Rockwell. Crockett turned narrowed eyes on me. "So you're back with him again?" The disapproval in his voice stirred my temper. "Didn't you get enough of the Seaforths the first time around?"

"Don't start with me," I hissed, keeping my voice low so Sam couldn't hear.

"Why not? You rag on me constantly."

"Everything okay?" Sam approached. His wary gaze flicked from me to Crockett and back to me again.

"Hey, Sammy." Crockett lifted his chin in greeting. "Long time no see."

"Crockett." Sam stared back at him but didn't offer his hand.

"Well, I'm out, boy scouts. See you around." Crockett turned his back to us and ambled down the street at a casual pace. I tracked him with my gaze as far as I could until he turned the corner, and wondered with a bitter pang if I'd ever see him again.

Chapter 15

Dakota

WHEN I'D WARNED Sam about John MacGruder, I'd meant every word of it. He was shrewd, savvy, and every bit as dangerous as Sam when it came to business. Beneath MacGruder's civil exterior lurked a man accustomed to winning. Sam had backed him into a corner, and MacGruder wouldn't lie down without a fight.

Over coffee and pastries, the three of us sat in the conference room of MacGruder & Sons. The polite conversation was over, and the war had begun.

"I've changed my mind," John said. "Deal's off."

"We shook hands. You can't back out now," Sam replied, tone quiet and easy.

To the untrained eye, the two men seemed friendly, casual. MacGruder leaned back in his seat, one arm thrown over the back of the empty chair beside him. He rested an ankle on his opposite knee. Sam loosened his tie then lifted his coffee cup to take a drink. The room crackled with testosterone and animosity, enough to lift the tiny hairs on the back of my neck.

"Handshakes don't mean shit. Pardon the language, Dakota," John said with a small nod in my direction. "You know that, Sam. The only thing I agreed upon was to listen to your proposal."

Sam shrugged. "You're still in a tight spot. You either have to sell to me or let my father ruin you. It's just a matter of time."

The set of MacGruder's mouth tightened. He ran a finger around the rim of his coffee cup. "So you're drawing a line in the sand? Either join up with you or fall to him? Frankly, I don't like any of those options."

"Look, John." Sam leaned forward, features earnest. "My dad plans to drive you into the ground and take this company for nothing."

"You know what I think?" John's face grew redder with each passing moment. "I think he sent you here to do his dirty work. Good cop, bad cop. You make the sweet offer. He makes the hard threats. Either way, he wins. And I'll tell you right now, I'd rather go down in a ball of fiery flames than roll over and die to either one of you." He slammed his fist on the table with so much force my coffee cup jumped on its saucer. I bit my lower lip and began to doodle in the margin of the paper.

"Look. I'd rather have you on board with this, but I don't need your permission to take you over." The steely edge in Sam's voice made my head snap up. I was a combination of impressed and repulsed by this latest side of him. "I'm giving you a choice on how this is going to go down."

"Don't threaten me." John's voice shook. "You're not your father. I don't owe you anything, and I sure as shit am not scared of you." He stood, his chair scraping across the floor like nails on a chalkboard. "Now, I think it's time for you to go."

Sam stood. Both men eyed each other, shoulders squared and chests expanded. It would've been comical if it hadn't been so frightening.

"Wait." I put a hand on John's sleeve. He glanced down at me, having forgotten I was even there.

Sam frowned. "Let's go, Dakota," he said. "We're done here."

"I don't think so," I said, amazed by my own boldness.

Sam's eyes blazed down at me, full of warning. His head shook by the slightest degree, imperceptible to anyone but me.

I bumbled forward anyway. I turned to John. "Sam's right. You're in a tight spot. If you don't sell out, you're going to go under. I've looked at all the properties you're sitting on, their demographics, the comp studies. You lost your ass on the last couple of deals."

"Dakota." John's eyes narrowed. Between his warning glare and Sam's growing irritation, I was treading on shaky ground. "I appreciate your--"

"Just hear me out," I interrupted. "Maybe there's a way for both of you to get what you want."

"Will you excuse us for a minute?" Sam gripped my elbow and pulled me out of the room and into the hallway. I trotted on tiptoe beside him, cheeks burning with humiliation. Once outside the room, he trapped me against the wall, eyes brimming with green fire. "What the hell are you doing, Dakota? I've got him right where I want him."

"He's throwing us out. I wouldn't call it a success." I yanked my arm from his grip and stared back at him, jaw jutted in defiance.

"It's part of the game. I lowball him. He turns me down. Next week, he'll be begging for a new offer." Sam cast a fake smile at the admin walking past us, but his anger returned the second she turned the corner. He bent, nose inches from mine, and spoke in a harsh whisper. "Let me run my business. What part of that don't you get?"

"You're screwing it up," I hissed. "He's not like other people. I'm telling you, if we walk out this door, he's not going to give us another chance."

We glared at each other, chests heaving with conviction and attraction. The starch from his shirt mingled with the scents of shower gel and cologne. I drew in a heady lungful. This combination, along with the fire in his eyes, caused my panties to dampen. In spite of our dispute, I was more turned on than I'd been in ages. I wanted to fist a hand in his hair and yank his mouth to mine for a hot, wet kiss.

His gaze dipped to my lips then lifted to my eyes. He looked inside me, so deep I felt naked and alone in an office full of people. My bones liquefied from the intensity of his scrutiny and the certainty that he was just as turned on as I was.

"You'd better not fuck this up," he said, drawing up to his full height. He tugged on the cuffs of his shirt and exhaled.

"And what if I do?" I lifted my chin, faking the confidence I didn't feel. "Are you going to spank me?"

"You'd like that, wouldn't you?" A hint of amusement curved his amazing lips. He touched a finger to the tip of my nose. "Maybe I will."

"Have a little faith." I smoothed a hand over his lapel, trying to hide the surge of triumph rushing through my veins like a drug. "Just sit back and let me do my thing."

Chapter 16

Sam

THE CAR GLIDED silently along the streets. Dakota sat in the corner, arms crossed over her chest, facing the window. I pretended to be checking emails on my phone, but I was really dissecting the emotions flicking across her face. They ranged in rapid succession from irritation and anger to embarrassment and disappointment. I could tell by the way she held her lower lip between her teeth that she was bracing for my wrath. Dakota had said her piece to MacGruder. He'd listened politely then asked us to leave. She thought she'd failed when in fact, she'd been brilliant. She'd suggested we work together, that maybe MacGruder might want to unload some of his properties in exchange for retaining control of a portion of his business.

Dakota, being smart as well as pretty, had figured out what each of us needed from the deal. I needed MacGruder's land to squelch my father's stadium deal. MacGruder needed cold, hard cash to save his business. What Dakota didn't know was that I'd leveraged every one of my personal assets and a few of Infinity's to buy out MacGruder. By suggesting a compromise, she might have saved me from bankruptcy.

I should've been panicked about my financial situation, but I'd learned long ago that the biggest risks resulted in the biggest payoffs. I was desperate for revenge. And as Malcolm Seaforth always said, a man with nothing to lose was the most dangerous of all adversaries. I had nothing to lose, and I was desperate as they came.

I let Dakota stew on her aggravation for a few miles, certain she'd be unable to maintain silence for long. Nothing turned me on more than her fire. She never backed down from a good fight, even when she was wrong. When we were married, we'd fought hard and fucked harder. She shifted twice, the leather creaking beneath her with each movement. At last, she snorted through her nose, an adorable noise of irritation, and turned to face me.

"Well, go ahead," she said. "I know you're dying to say it."

"Say what?" I asked, looking up from my phone.

"I told you so." She wrinkled her nose.

"I told you so," I replied and returned my gaze to the phone, biting back a smile.

"Is that it? No lecture? No big speech about letting you run your business?"

"Nope." I continued tapping out the reply to a group text from Beckett and Tucker, requesting my presence at the bar later for drinks.

"I thought you were going to make me pay." Her voice held a note of anxiety mixed with interest.

Sexual electricity hummed between us. My gaze drifted to her leg, the long stretch of trim calf, her slender ankle, followed by a vision of how those legs would feel wrapped around my waist. "I will." I liked keeping her on edge and, by the flush of her cheeks, she liked it too. "You can take that to the bank."

"When?" She inched closer until our knees touched.

"Later." I kept my head down, smiling while she huffed.

"I hope I didn't ruin everything. I really thought I had it."

In spite of my best efforts, I couldn't resist taking her by the chin and pressing my lips to hers. She tasted sweet, like cotton candy. It was her lip gloss. When we parted, I licked my lips, savoring the sweetness, my cock instantly hard. "It'll be fine." I spoke with conviction, but my chest tightened with anxiety. How could I convince her when I couldn't even convince myself?

The car stopped. Rockwell came around to open my door. I got out, Dakota behind me, and came face to face with Dahlia. Her gaze lingered on my lips for an inappropriate amount of time before flicking to Dakota. She nodded in greeting then moved inside the building. I'd known Dahlia long enough to know something was on her mind, and I had a feeling it wasn't good.

I'd barely settled into my office when Dahlia appeared. With so many things on my mind, I didn't have time for Dahlia and her petty games. I was eager to get back to the business of business.

"What's up?" I asked while powering up my computer. "Make it quick."

"What's going on with you and Dakota?" She didn't sit but stood in front of my desk, arms folded over her chest like a shield.

"Nothing." A quick flash of guilt swept through me, the same way I'd felt when I was caught stealing cookies from the kitchen as a kid. Only this time, I hadn't stolen anything. I had taken what was mine, and it felt damn good.

"You've got lip gloss all over your mouth." She grabbed a tissue from the dispenser on the corner of my desk and held it out to me.

I didn't take it. Instead, I ran my tongue over my lower lip, savoring again the lingering taste of Dakota's mouth on mine. "Not your business, Dahlia," I said, returning my attention to the flood of emails pouring into my inbox.

"It is my business when half the office knows what you're doing with her. I mean, really, Sam? You bring her to work every day. Rockwell takes her home at night. I turned a blind eye to the interns, but this is getting out of hand. At least you stayed under the radar with the others."

"Once again, not your business," I replied, feeling the sting of irritation.

"I'm only saying this as a friend. You don't want a sexual harassment lawsuit, do you?" She shook her head, an expression of disappointment on her face.

I sighed and sat back in my chair, closing my eyes for a few seconds to gather my thoughts. She wasn't going to give up, and worst of all, she was right. The other employees were already talking; rumors were circulating. I'd seen the way they ignored Dakota and heard their whispers whenever we walked by.

"She's my ex-wife." The confession slipped out much more easily than I'd anticipated. This was huge. I felt lighter almost immediately. The sooner everyone knew, the sooner I could quit pretending Dakota meant nothing to me.

"You mean she's *the one*?" The look of shocked disbelief on Dahlia's face would've been comical if it had been any other circumstance. "Sam? What in the hell are you thinking?"

"I'm thinking this conversation is over." I returned my attention to the computer monitor. "Shut the door on your way out, would you?"

Chapter 17

Dakota

WHEN I GOT home that evening, I found Crockett sitting in the hallway, leaning against my apartment door. His clothes were smeared with dirt. A limp, greasy lock of his hair hung over one eye. I sniffed the air and winced when I got close.

"You stink," I said, waving a hand in front of my face.

"And you're ugly, but I still love you," he replied. He got to his feet and watched while I unlocked the door. "Can I come in?"

"Did you get a job?" I stared warily at him, torn between doing the right thing or the easy thing. Part of me wanted to give him a hug, tell him everything would be okay, and make us dinner. Another part of me knew I would only be inviting trouble for the both of us if I let him in.

"No." He edged toward the door.

"Then you can't stay here." I blocked his approach.

"Jesus, Kota. One more night. I'm serious." He pushed his hair back from his face, a petulant furrow on his forehead, the same expression he'd worn as a six-year-old. "I could really use a shower. Besides, it's going to rain, and I don't feel well." A peculiar shade of green tinged his complexion, and his eyes were dull, devoid of their usual sky blue.

"Okay. Fine." I stepped aside. A bright smile bowed his lips, and my hopes plummeted, knowing he'd once again played me. He pushed past me and into the living room. "But this is the last time. Tomorrow you're going to the mission and see if you can get a room there."

"I hate the mission," he shouted from the bathroom. I heard the water turn on and the banging of cabinet doors as he searched for a towel. "They make you pray twice a day."

"Good. You need to pray, you big sinner," I shouted in reply.

He stuck his head out the door, shoulders bare. Steam rolled into the hallway. "People who live in glass houses, Kota."

I made macaroni and cheese from a box, heated a can of green beans and a few smoked sausages for our dinner. We ate at the table and laughed about silly things. He helped me wash and dry the dishes. Later, we played Scrabble until we were both bleary-eyed. It was one of the best times together I could remember since we'd reached adulthood.

"I'm going into rehab tomorrow afternoon," he announced in the middle of our board game. I stopped, hand in midair holding a letter tile. He rolled his eyes. "Don't make a big deal out of it."

"It is a big deal." In spite of his protests, I threw my arms around him and held him tightly. "This is great. I'm so happy for you. What brought this about?"

One of his shoulders lifted and fell in a shrug. "I think I'm out of options."

Relief washed over me. A weight I hadn't known I carried dropped from my chest. "You've been before. What makes this any different?" I'd seen him fail on three previous attempts to get clean. As much as I wanted to believe this time was different, my excitement was tempered by trepidation.

"One of my friends died from an overdose last week." His expression twisted with the first sincere remorse I'd seen in years.

"I'm sorry." I covered his hand with mine, tears of empathy stinging my eyes.

"It could've been me. I don't want to be that guy, Kota."

The thought of losing him like that constricted my chest with panic. Yet it was entirely possible. Over the past few years, I'd steeled myself for the possibility, dreading the day I received the phone call announcing my brother was dead from an overdose or a drug deal gone wrong. "I don't want to lose you, Crockett. Neither does Mom."

His sheepish grin warmed my heart. "It's a place outside of the city. They take a few charity cases every year, so it won't cost anything."

"This is good, Crockett. So good." I covered his hand with mine and squeezed. Pink colored his cheeks. "Does Mom know?"

"Yeah. I called her this morning." We hugged again.

"Do you need a ride there?" I choked back tears of relief and happiness, knowing he wouldn't appreciate the show of emotion.

"Nah, I'm good," was all he said.

After midnight, I crept from my bed to watch him sleep. He looked so young and vulnerable, his dark hair mussed, eyelashes fanned over his cheeks. His skin stretched over the bones of his face, and he was too pale. I curled my fingers into fists, wanting to hug him one more time and somehow make all his problems go away. But they were his problems to solve, and it was his life to live. I had enough issues of my own with Sam.

In the morning, thunder rattled the windows of the apartment. I didn't have the heart to throw Crockett into the midst of a storm, so I let him stay after I left for work. I offered to see if Rockwell would drop him at the bus station, but he declined the option in order to sleep a few more hours. He promised to leave as soon as the weather cleared, and I chose to believe him.

Chapter 18

Dakota

A LITTLE PAST ten in the morning, Samuel summoned me to his office. I hadn't seen him yet. He'd arrived early for a call to Tokyo. Rockwell had driven me into the office. A thrill of anticipation buzzed through me, the way it did every time I saw Sam. When I entered, he was pacing the length of the room, Bluetooth in one ear, conversing in French with someone on the other end of the line. He didn't glance in my direction, just waved me toward the conference table opposite his desk. By the time he ended the call, my nerves were dancing.

"Are you ready?" he asked. As he spoke, he strode to the door then clicked the lock. Rain drizzled down the windowpanes, the drops creating a pleasant pattering noise.

"For what?" Moisture began to gather on my palms. I'd seen that look in his eyes before, pupils black as onyx, and knew it meant either one of two things. Either he was pissed or he was horny. I expected the first but hoped for the second.

He pushed the intercom, gaze locked with mine, promising me things--dirty, hot things. My nipples drew tight beneath the white silk of my blouse. "Mrs. Cantrell, please hold all my calls. Make sure we're not disturbed."

I swallowed hard. Could he be any more handsome this morning? He wore a dark gray pinstripe suit with a tan vest beneath and a crisp, white dress shirt. The scruff on his cheeks had been trimmed into a beard outlining his square jaw. It gave him a somber, commanding air. It gave *me* heart palpitations.

"You didn't answer me. I want to know if you're ready. For your punishment." As he spoke, he went to the door and turned the lock. It clicked, echoing inside my ears like a gunshot. "From yesterday."

"Excuse me?" A white-hot thrill shot through my body. I had the MacGruder file in my grasp, prepared for another grueling session of numbers and data. I wasn't prepared for whatever glimmered in his eyes.

"Put your hands on the table," he said, his voice low and deep.

"What?" A tendril of hair escaped its hairpin. I puffed it away, trembling too hard to risk repairing it.

"You heard me, Ms. Atwell." He came around the end of the table to stand behind me. The heat of his breath shimmered over the shell of my ear, sending ripples of gooseflesh along my neck. "Do it. Now."

"So bossy, Mr. Seaforth," I chided, but I did as I was told. Cool air whispered across my thighs as I bent over the table. With my palms flat on the walnut surface, I cast a questioning glance over my shoulder. His gaze rested on mine. What I saw there winded me. Playful. Confident. Demanding. All the things he'd been when I'd married him. All the things I needed him to be in the present.

"You, Ms. Atwell, are insubordinate and headstrong. What am I going to do with you?"

"Well, you could start by giving me a raise," I countered.

One large hand skimmed over the back of my knee then surged upward along the inside of my thigh. His thumb halted just short of my panties. "You don't even have a job here yet," he murmured, voice rough. "And after that little escapade yesterday? Well, you've got a lot of balls to ask for more money. You'll be lucky to make it through the day here."

A wave of panic replaced the lust welling inside me, the way it did every time the subject turned to money. I silently cursed myself for bringing up the subject. His hand gripped my thigh, warm and demanding my attention. I forgot to worry when his thumb stroked the tender flesh on the inside of my leg, grateful I'd worn my favorite bra and panties today. I could hardly wait until he saw them.

"I've been thinking, Ms. Atwell. Maybe it's time we take this relationship to the next level." The fly of his trousers pressed against the cleft of my bottom, giving me a good idea of what awaited me. He ran a hand along the groove of my spine. I closed my eyes, savoring each second of his touch, impatient for more. My thighs twitched to ease the ache between them. After a few short seconds, he backed away. The chill of air conditioning replaced his body heat.

"I'm open for negotiations. What did you have in mind?" I looked over my shoulder at him and started to stand up, removing my hands from the table.

"Hands on the table."

The low, warning growl of his voice did incredible things to my insides. I complied, loving this new game. So full of surprises, my Samuel. I could see his reflection in that god-awful, ostentatious mirror on the opposite wall. He pulled a chair from the table and placed it behind me, sliding into it with his easy grace. "You're so fucking hot like this, Kota. I'm just going to sit here and admire you for a minute." He dragged his palm over his zipper, exaggerating the outline of his erection. My insides clenched, so turned on by his desire for me that I could barely stand still.

"Wait until you see what I'm wearing underneath," I said and widened my stance a little further. It was an uncomfortable position in four-inch heels. With my hands on the table and my ass in the air, it created an ache in my back. If it turned him on, I was willing to take one for the team, however.

"Show me."

"I'll have to take my hands off the table." My pulse tripped and my palms began to sweat with nervous anticipation.

"Go ahead."

With seeming leisure, I turned to face him. While he watched with lust-darkened eyes, I trailed a finger down the placket of my blouse. His gaze followed along as I popped each button. Beneath the silk shirt, I wore a white lace bra, my breasts surging upward in perky abandon. Pink satin bows adorned the straps and centered between the cups. I let my shirt open before shrugging out of it. Sam's chest rose and fell, rose and fell, with two deep breaths.

"Keep going." He twirled a finger in the air, one brow cocked.

"You said you wanted to negotiate the terms of our relationship. What was it you had in mind?" I turned my back to him, fingers gripping the hem of my skirt, and pulled it up high enough to reveal my panties. They were sheer white lace in front. The backside consisted of several delicate beaded strands gathered from the hip to the center, joined by a matching bow, exposing the whole of my bottom.

"Damn," he muttered. "You wear that fucking shit to work?" Sam rarely swore. He said profanity was for people with low IQs and limited vocabulary. I guessed my lingerie had that effect on him.

"I like wearing sexy things," I said, letting the skirt drop back into place before turning to face him once more. "It makes me feel like I have a secret."

"That's one hell of a secret, sweet pea." He scratched his jaw, fingernails rasping on the wiry hairs. "If I'd known you were dressed like that, I would've cancelled my meetings this morning."

I crooked a finger at him. "Come here, sexy man." The corners of his mouth turned up in a devilish grin. "Let's negotiate."

Chapter 19

Dakota

SAM CROSSED THE room in two long strides. His mouth found mine, lips softer than I remembered, even though it had only been a day since our last kiss. The plush hairs of his new beard tickled my chin. I fisted my fingers into his shirt, drawing him closer, savoring the scent of his shampoo and the cologne he always wore. He tasted of coffee and cinnamon pastry. The tactile sensations were sweet, familiar reminders of lazy morning lovemaking and frenzied late-night fucks.

He kissed me like it was the first time and the last time, like he wanted me, like he loved me. My tummy twittered when his fingers tightened on my hips. The sweep of his tongue over mine was more than a kiss, it was a claiming, a statement that he was mine and I was his and nothing would ever change those facts.

"Strip," he murmured when we finally parted. "Leave the panties on."

I quickly complied, watching while he unbuttoned his shirt. Ripples of muscle covered his abdomen. A trail of dark blond hair disappeared into the waistband of his trousers. He unbuckled his belt, unbuttoned the fly, and lowered the zipper. When he hesitated, I drew him forward, centering him between my legs. I tugged his boxers down, and his erection bobbed forward, long and heavy.

"I've imagined this so many times," he said, skimming a hand down my throat. "Fucking you on the table. Here. Like this." His palm rested between my breasts. I could feel my heart thumping against it in uneven, excited beats.

"Me too," I whispered, barely able to speak past the knot in my throat. I wanted to tell him how much I'd missed him, but something kept me from saying the words. I needed to know how he felt before I put myself out there, and I was too much a coward to ask.

"Put this on me." He pressed a foil packet into my palm.

I tore it open with my teeth and unrolled the condom over his length. When I was finished, he pulled aside the crotch of my panties, exposing my sex. We both looked down to where the tip of his cock nudged my clit. It was hot, sexy, and the most erotic thing I'd ever seen. He dragged the head of his erection along my wetness, preparing me for him.

"No foreplay. I need you," I managed to say on a ragged exhale. I was drenched and ready for him. Standing in front of him made my heart pound and my mouth dry.

"Sweetheart, every minute with you is foreplay for me." He pressed into me slowly with a quiet moan, one centimeter at a time, drawing out the pleasure of two becoming one. Our eyes met. Suddenly I was drawn into the depths of the man in front of me, tumbling through grass-green irises into the convoluted soul of my ex-husband.

The hands on my hips were warm, holding me in place, demanding my compliance. I surrendered willingly while he moved in and out of me, in and out, in and out. He surged inside with agonizing delay, dragging out to the tip before easing in to the root again.

"I've missed you, baby."

The sweet confession melted all of my doubts, liquefied my bones, and dissolved any resistance I might have had. "I know. I missed you, too." When I cupped his cheek, he turned his face into my palm and planted a kiss in the center.

"This is good, right?" The uncertainty in his question had me searching his eyes. They were filled with naked need and vulnerability. "This is more than fucking, isn't it?"

"Oh, Sam." Tears stung my eyes. His words broke my heart and shored it up, all at the same time. He wanted to love me again, but something held him back. I knew it was the hurt of my betrayal. I could heal the wound if he'd let me. I'd give anything to take away his uncertainty. "It was always more. It's still more."

He rested his forehead against mine. We moved together, nose to nose, lips to lips, breathing and feeling, savoring the sweet ache of our union. Pleasure built with an intensity bordering on pain. I slipped my hands beneath his shirt, tracing the smooth groove of his spine, letting him set the pace while I worshipped him with soft touches and tiny, tender kisses.

"If I wanted to take care of you, would you let me?" I asked, burying my face into his neck. I felt him stiffen and feared I'd gone too far, ruining our moment of intimacy.

"You want to?" With fingers tangled in my hair, he pulled my head back, tipping my face up to meet his. The flare of his nostrils sent a new pulse of need through me. Something possessive and masculine sparked in his eyes. "Do you want to be mine, Dakota?"

"Yes." It was all I ever wanted.

With my confession, the nature of our sex changed. He shoved into me hard enough to make me gasp. "Can I trust you?" He thrust into me again, bruising and punishing me with each stroke, eyes filled with a wild, primeval light.

"Yes." I fought back the tears threatening to spill over at any second and clung to him. "I promise, Sam."

"You promised once before. How do I know you mean it this time?"

"Because now I know how much it hurts to live without you." Our gazes held fast. I took his face between my palms to show him my sincerity. "There will never be anyone else for me, Sam. You're my one and only."

Something inside him released. He pushed me down, the wood cold and unyielding against my back. One of his hands hooked my right leg over his hip. The rhythm of his thrusts increased until he was pounding into me. Our skin slapped together. The friction of his erection against my clit ignited tiny explosions of bliss inside my core. I rose to meet him, wishing I could draw him further inside me, keep him safe, and never let him go.

He tilted my pelvis, angling deeper. I couldn't breathe, couldn't think, couldn't stop myself from clinging to him. I came hard, fingernails digging into his ass, teeth buried in his shoulder. My sex fluttered and pulsed around him. Each spasm sent ripples of fiery ecstasy to the tips of my toes. My legs trembled with the strength of each contraction. His muted grunts of pleasure spurred my orgasm. It went on and on while he rode me faster.

"You've always belonged to me," he hissed. I opened my eyes to find his face inches from mine, etched with need. My body continued to clutch and spasm around his, filling me with a euphoria I hadn't known possible. He slowed long enough to press a tender kiss on the tip of my nose. "You just didn't know it."

Chapter 20

Dakota

AFTER WORK THAT day, at Sam's insistence, I found myself on the steps of Le Beau Monde, an exclusive dress shop on the elite side of the city. I took Muriel with me for fortification, having never ventured into that kind of place before. Once I'd broken the news to her about Sam's invitation to accompany him to the Charity Auction, she'd recovered from her shock with impressive speed. She was happy to ride in the BMW with Rockwell behind the wheel. He dropped us at the front door with his cell number in case we couldn't find a taxi home. I didn't care what Muriel thought. I floated on a cloud of euphoria, still sated and glowing from sex with Sam.

Inside Le Beau Monde, we sat on velvet chairs beneath glittering gold chandeliers in a private room, sipping champagne and nibbling some kind of hard sugar cookie while waiting for the owner to greet us. A tall, thin brunette floated into the room on endlessly long legs. She gazed down her nose at us, obviously unimpressed by my box store suit. "Did you say someone referred you?"

"Yes. Samuel Seaforth?" I handed her Sam's business card, the one with Le Beau Monde's address written on the back. She turned it over between fingers tipped in taupe polish. "He said to ask for Fran."

The brunette eyed me again then disappeared into the back room to retrieve her employer. In my mind, I pictured Fran as an elderly woman with regal gray hair swept into a twist, powdered cheeks, and elegant hands. I had not pictured a knockout redhead in her late twenties, wearing vintage Chanel and sporting lush curves worthy of a centerfold.

"Dakota." Fran came at me on legs like an Amazon, a diamond-encrusted hand extended in greeting. "I've been expecting you."

Several things hit me at once with unpleasant force. First, this was the woman from the Internet, the one hugging Sam's arm in the paparazzi photos. The hairs at the nape of my neck bristled with animosity and jealousy at the realization. And second, there was something disturbingly familiar about her, something I couldn't quite put a finger on.

"Hi. Thank you for seeing me," I said, curbing the desire to turn tail and run. The bones of her hand felt fragile in my grasp even though she topped my five-ten frame by several inches.

"You don't remember me," she said, regarding me with breathtaking blue eyes. I took a second, more discerning look at her features, the short, straight nose, high forehead, and decided mouth. A vision of a gawky, freckle-faced teenager flashed through my memories.

I took a step back, mouth agape. "Clover?"

She nodded, her smile growing larger and more beautiful. "Yes. It's Fran now. I go by my middle name." She tightened her grip on my hand. "Clover's just embarrassing, don't you think?" Genuine warmth suffused her tone. "It's been forever, hasn't it?"

Clover had been a few years behind me in high school. Although her family owned a prolific chain of department stores across the nation, she'd been awkward and unattractive back then, made all the more pathetic by her blatant infatuation with Sam. He'd been oblivious to her, but I remembered the way she'd blushed every time he'd looked her way.

I forced a smile, trying to swallow my dismay at finding her so gorgeous. "Yes, it has." I pried my hand from hers. Muriel nudged my elbow for an introduction. "Um, this is my friend Muriel."

"It's a pleasure to meet you, Muriel. Please make yourself comfortable," Fran said, nodding toward the silver tray of refreshments. She turned back to face me. "When Sam told me at breakfast yesterday that you were going to the auction with him, I nearly choked on my bagel."

Breakfast? Fran continued talking, but my mind clung to the one word with inane stubbornness. They'd had breakfast together? Yesterday? He'd said he had an early call from Tokyo. Knots of turmoil formed in my belly as I tried to make sense of the situation.

"I'm sorry. Back up a minute. You had breakfast together yesterday?" I interrupted her diatribe, trying to find my way through the fog in my brain.

"Oh, yes. We have breakfast every other week. We have for years. It's kind of a ritual," she said with a wave of her manicured hand. "Can I just say I always thought you two were perfect together?"

My gaze met Muriel's. She lifted an eyebrow as if to say, *I told you so*, and returned to laying waste to the platter of cookies.

"It was a long time ago." I heard my voice from far away, thin and high-pitched. "We've only just reconnected."

"I felt terrible, cancelling on him at the last minute," Fran said. "I'm so glad you're able to go with him in my place."

Sam had an ongoing relationship with this stunning woman, a woman who possessed all the qualities I'd never have? The revelation hit me in the gut like a prizefighter's punch. Fran was from a good family--the best, cultured, successful, and smart. I'd thought he'd invited me to the auction as a date, but as it turned out, I was only a replacement for someone else. All my warm, fuzzy feelings from earlier in the day withered and died in the dressing room at Le Beau Monde. I felt foolish and gullible and confused. I'd been so convinced Sam still loved me that I'd forgotten the other women from his past. My insecurities flared, bigger and brighter than ever. How could he possibly love me over this scintillating creature?

"You know, I'm not feeling so well," I said. It wasn't a lie. The hamburger from the bar down the street churned in my stomach and threatened to come back up every time I pictured Sam with Fran. "I think I'm going to go."

"Oh?" Fran's mouth drooped with disappointment. "I've got some great gowns for you. Are you sure? It'll only take a few minutes."

I glanced at Muriel, hoping for backup, but she had her cellphone glued to her ear. She waved an encouraging hand at me then disappeared outside to continue her conversation.

Fran took my silence as acquiescence and began pulling dresses from the rack. "What about this one? It'll make the color of your eyes pop. They're such an amazing shade of aquamarine. Do you wear tinted lenses?" Fran held a gown up to my chest, her critical gaze sweeping my figure from head to toe. "Try this one on."

A few minutes later, I stood in the changing room, wearing the gown, unable to think of anything but Sam. I knew he was arrogant, but this latest move exceeded my greatest expectations. He'd sent me to his lover's shop to procure a dress. What kind of guy did something like that? Especially after the intimacy we'd shared earlier today. The more I thought about it, the angrier and more hurt I became. By the time I changed into the second dress, I'd worked myself into a snit. The nerve of him. Hell would freeze over before I went anywhere with him, especially the auction. I picked up my cellphone and punched in his number. He answered on the second ring.

"Hey, baby." I heard the sound of male voices in the background mingled with music.

"Don't *hey, baby* me," I snapped. "I can't believe you sent me to Clover for a dress. Your lover? Really, Sam."

"What?" Laughter tinged his voice. The sound sent a tingle of attraction between my legs. Damn traitorous hoo-ha. I squelched the feeling by picturing Clover on his arm.

"I saw your pictures on the Internet. I know you were seeing her. And you sent me here?" I struggled to keep the volume of my voice at a calm level, knowing Fran--Clover--whatever the hell she called herself--was outside the room.

"Dakota." The laughter had stopped, and I heard a note of concern in my name.

"You asked her to the auction before me," I said, sounding like a whiny brat and hating myself for it.

"Yes, but--"

"That was a dick move, Sam," I shouted into the phone. "Even for you."

I didn't wait to hear his response. I ended the call and stuffed the phone back into my purse. The zipper on the dress snagged as I tried to escape the tulle. I struggled to release it, contorting into positions my yoga instructor would be proud of, with no avail. After a few minutes of my grunting and snorting, Fran slid the heavy velvet curtain to the side. Her sleek eyebrows lifted. I was drenched with sweat. One lock of my hair hung over my eye. Both my arms were trapped inside the dress, which I'd tried unsuccessfully to pull over my head.

"Let me help you," she said.

I stood immobile while she repaired the zipper. The heat of my anger dissipated and left me feeling deflated. As she tugged the dress over my head, I avoided eye contact, embarrassed by my outburst.

"I appreciate your time," I said and stepped into my own dress, preparing to leave. I wanted to get as far away from her and her perfection as I could. "It seems I won't be needing a dress after all."

"Please." She touched my arm. I lifted my eyes reluctantly to find her expression kind. Why did she have to be so nice? It would be much easier to hate her if she was a shrew. "I couldn't help but overhear. I think you've got the wrong idea."

"No. I've got exactly the right idea," I replied. My anger began to rejuvenate. "If you don't mind, would you call us a taxi?"

Twenty minutes later, we were still waiting on the cab. Muriel grew impatient and took the first bus, claiming she had a date with the guy next door to her apartment, leaving me alone on the sidewalk. I didn't care. It gave me time to think. Once my temper had cooled for the second time, I began to feel foolish. Perhaps I had overreacted to Sam's relationship with Fran. If he had feelings for her, he wouldn't have sent me to her shop. Or would he? It was exactly the kind of mind game Malcolm Seaforth would play. The thought made me queasy. I didn't want to think Sam was like his dad, but I had to admit the possibility.

I wrapped my arms around my waist, chilled in spite of the warm air, and scanned the street for the next bus. Apparently, taxis were in high demand on this particular evening. My gaze fell on a red Porsche instead, fenders gleaming, chrome wheels glinting in the sun as it rounded the street corner. A jolt of excitement and dread buzzed through me. I put my head down and started walking in the opposite direction. From behind me, I heard a car door slam and footsteps on the sidewalk.

"Kota," Sam's voice called after me. I kept walking, unprepared for a confrontation. He caught my arm by the bicep and turned me to face him. I stared at the tips of his boots. "What's going on?"

"I'm waiting for a cab."

"Fran called me. She said you were upset--as if I didn't know by the way you hung up on me." I heard a tinge of amusement in his words laced with something akin to panic. "Care to share?"

"I don't like being sloppy seconds." I tried to tug my arm from his grasp, but his fingers curled tighter.

"What are you talking about?" The frank curiosity in his gaze eased a little of my distress, but I was too stubborn to concede without a fight.

"She was your date to the auction. You only asked me because she couldn't go."

A muscle ticked below his cheekbone. He glared, eyes narrowing. "I did ask her first."

I threw my hands in the air and started walking again without destination, anywhere to get away from him. He followed on my heels.

"She cancelled. I asked you. What's the big deal?" This time when he reached for my arm, I shot him a look of fire and brimstone.

"You are such a guy." Several passersby turned to look at me and made a wide berth around us. I lowered my voice to an acceptable level and continued, "Why did you ask me then? Because I was easy? Because you couldn't get anyone else at the last minute?"

"I asked you because you're smart, pretty, and an asset to the business." He blew out an exasperated breath and shoved his hands into his pants pockets. "I didn't ask you before because we were divorced and barely on speaking terms. Hell, it's only been two weeks, Kota. And you've got to admit, it's been a rollercoaster ride."

Of course, he was right and I was wrong. Again. I crossed my arms over my chest and stared at him, desperately searching for a way to make myself look less foolish. "The point is you asked *her*." We were in front of the shop again. I gestured to the door. "I know you fucked *other consenting adults*," I said, throwing his words back at him from our first car ride together, "but I don't want to see them face to face."

"It's not like that," he began, but I cut him off.

"You mean to tell me you haven't slept with her?"

Hesitation and guilt flickered in his eyes then anger and frustration flared to replace them. "Oh, for the love of God." He opened the shop door and gave me a little shove over the threshold. Fran looked up from behind the counter, eyebrow raised. "Talk some sense into her, would you? The way things are going, I might strangle her."

"I tried," Fran said with a shake of her fiery mane. She glided around the counter to stand beside Sam and placed a hand on his arm. Their eyes met, and my insides shriveled at the shared admiration in their gazes. "She's very stubborn."

"Like a mule," Sam muttered.

Fran patted Sam's arm. A vision of them naked in bed, perfect bodies entwined, scalded my psyche. Mortification heated my cheeks. I looked away, wounded by their intimacy. He was mine. All mine. And I didn't intend to share him with anyone.

"Dakota, I'm gay," Fran said.

My jaw went slack.

"She's a lesbian," Sam said. "I turned her gay."

Relief washed over me, intense and immediate. I barked out a laugh, startled by the admission and Sam's look of embarrassment.

"You did not," Fran reprimanded and shoved him playfully. "I just wasn't ready to come out yet."

"Well, it sure seemed that way," he replied. "So yes, Dakota, we've slept together."

"It was horrible," Fran said with an apologetic glance to Sam. "I mean, for both of us, I think." Sam rolled his eyes, but a reluctant grin curved his mouth. "I'm sure we would both rather forget it ever happened."

"Yes. Let's do that," Sam said. "I was so traumatized I couldn't get it up for a month afterward."

Fran shoved him again, and they both laughed.

"Somehow I doubt that," I murmured, trying to ignore the tumultuous flip in my stomach. Discussing Sam's libido with another woman--a gorgeous woman--made me uneasy. Jealousy continued to spark and sputter through me.

"My family doesn't know," Fran said. "And I'd like to keep it that way." She gave Sam another smile, radiant and sweet. "Sam and I found it mutually agreeable to attend functions together. It took the pressure off both of us."

"Oh." I bit my lower lip, unable to find more words.

"I'm her beard," Sam said.

This time we all laughed. I admired their easy friendship, the way they seemed to like each other without the weight of sexual attraction.

Fran hooked an arm through Sam's elbow then mine. She tugged us toward the fitting rooms. "So, if we're all good here, let's get this show on the road. I've got just a few more dresses for you to try."

"But my cab." I gestured to the shop front and the street outside.

"I never called him," Fran admitted. "I called Sam instead."

"Nice," Sam said. "Very nice."

I stood in front of the three-way mirror in a silver gown, my back to Sam. The satin fabric was free from embellishment and fell to the floor in a flattering line from waist to hip. I found his reflection in the mirror. His eyes were glued to my ass. A flush warmed me from the inside out and settled into my cheeks.

"My eyes are up here, young man," I chided.

"I'll get there in a second," he replied without missing a beat. "Turn around."

I twirled slowly, enjoying the way the hem swirled around my toes. "What do you think?"

"This is definitely the one," he said. At long last his eyes met mine. They were heated, dark, and infinitely enigmatic. "Are you sure you don't want me to buy it for you?"

"I'm sure," I said, my breath stolen by his expression. "But thank you."

"No, thank you," he countered. "Watching you change clothes might be the sexiest thing I've ever seen."

"Then you don't get out much." I smiled at him, happy to see him happy.

"Everything good in here?" Fran popped her head inside the room, gaze flitting from Sam to me and back to Sam again.

"We're going to take this one," he said, his gaze still locked with mine. "Can we have a few minutes?"

"Sure." She smiled. "Take as long as you want. Shop closes at nine."

"You could have told me, you know," I said once she'd disappeared. "Instead of letting me think the worst."

"Do you really want a list of every woman I've slept with?" He made an ineffectual grab for my waist, but I stayed just out of his reach.

"Yes," I said then immediately recanted. "Well, no. Maybe not."

The idea of Sam with other women would never sit well with me. Ever. I slipped the straps of the gown down my shoulders, keeping my gaze locked with his, enjoying the way his jeans tented in the front. Apparently, he'd taken a clue from our date and procured a set of nicely faded Levi's. Paired with an untucked dress shirt and boots, the ensemble gave him a structured casual look.

"You were jealous." A smug smirk lit his features. "I liked it."

"You sure got yourself here in a hurry." I hiked the hem of the gown up to my thighs and straddled his lap. The brush of denim against my bare legs felt naughty and exciting.

"I was down the street having drinks with Tuck and Beckett." He ran his tongue over his lower lip, looking famished. My heart skipped a beat, knowing it was for me.

"Can you help me with the zipper on this?" I trailed my fingers over the buttons of his shirt, the heat of his chest warm beneath my touch. A reflexive shiver shook my body.

"Have you ever had sex in a dressing room?" His lips found my neck. The puff of his breath against the tender flesh excited all of my nerve endings, tingling down to my breasts and tightening my nipples.

"No." I arched my back and angled my head so he could kiss along my throat.

"Me neither," he said, words vibrating against me. "It'll be another first--for both of us."

Chapter 21

Dakota

ONCE A WEEK, I continued the hunt for my wedding ring. I'd worn it on a chain around my neck for an entire decade, until I'd lost it a few weeks ago. Now that things were heating up between Sam and me, I missed the symbol of our union more than ever. On Saturday, the day of the charity auction, I scoured the apartment, delving into nooks and crannies I hadn't seen in years. Two hours later, the place was in a shambles, sofa cushions upturned, drawers open, and clothing thrown askew. I had no idea where it might have gone.

By the time I finished my search, it was time to prepare for my date with Sam. If it was a date. I still wasn't sure where I stood with him, but the idea sent my pulse into all kinds of crazy dances. He was beginning to trust me, and after meeting Fran, I had high hopes for our future together.

Thanks to Fran, the gown looked spectacular. It was gathered in the right places to slim my curvy hips and emphasize my waist. I curled my hair with meticulous care and gathered the ringlets into a Grecian updo. Matching sandals and neutral makeup completed the look. I wanted to appear sexy but classy, knowing Sam would be the picture of sophistication.

When he arrived at my door, he didn't disappoint. He wore a black tuxedo with a gray pinstriped waistcoat and a silver tie the exact color of my dress. The appreciation in his eyes as they swept over me more than compensated for the state of anxiety I found myself in.

On legs of jelly, I wandered into the ballroom at Sam's side. He made an imposing sight with the inverted V of his broad shoulders and narrow hips draped in perfectly tailored Hugo Boss. Female eyes drifted over him admiringly, drawn by the contrast of his gold hair and tanned skin against the pristine white of his dress shirt. Pride tempered my trepidation. My boy had become a man and made a success of himself. I couldn't claim any responsibility for what he'd done, but my heart swelled at the knowledge just the same.

Dahlia spied Sam and made a beeline for him from across the room. When she saw me at his side, she stopped short. It was too late for her to turn back, however, and she met us halfway to our table. She avoided my gaze, focusing her attention on Sam.

"Is MacGruder here?" Sam asked, ignoring the furrow between her fair brows.

"Yes. He's with his son Jared." She managed a sweet smile for him. "I'm glad to see you finally made it. I was starting to worry. You're never late."

He didn't reply, and I saw the frank curiosity on her face at his lack of response. I admired that about him. He never felt the need to make excuses. He threaded his fingers through mine and pulled me toward our table. I jerked, surprised by the public display, but his fingers tightened.

"Come on," he said.

We were at a table of twelve with an enormous crystal vase full of white flowers in the center. Their sweet scents lingered in the air. John and Jared

MacGruder both stood when I arrived. Dahlia and an accountant-type guy were seated across from us, along with two more couples I didn't know. Sam pulled out my chair and took a seat beside me.

"Dakota, this is Beckett," Sam said, nodding to the first couple. A tall, athletic man with a crew cut stood and offered his hand. He bore an intimidating air of authority reinforced by his firm handshake. "And this is Tucker." The man beside Beckett nodded but didn't stand. He was hot in a messy, bad boy kind of way. One large foot extended into the aisle by my chair. I couldn't help noticing he wore black-and-white Chuck Taylors with his tuxedo or the blatant disapproval in his stare. My stomach churned with anxiety but I managed to give him a smile. Of course, his friends hated me. How could I expect any less? The warmth of Sam's palm against mine steadied my nerves. He gestured to the man beside Dahlia. "And this is Mark, head of accounting at Infinity."

When the introductions were over, I sank into my chair, exhausted by the pretense of the event. I had no idea how to act around his friends. Did they know about us? I tensed, afraid I might do or say something inappropriate. Sam seemed at home. He gave me a reassuring nod before turning to make conversation with John. A few seconds later, his hand found mine beneath the table and gave it a solid squeeze. Warmth suffused me, the way it did every time he touched me.

After the meal, I wandered through the auction items while Sam talked business. As he'd predicted, MacGruder had come back with a counteroffer not long after we'd left his office following our last meeting. Something he'd failed to mention during my *punishment* of the previous day.

Thoughts bounced around inside my head, and I tried to make sense out of all that had happened between us over the past few weeks. I traversed the length of the ballroom twice, drank two glasses of champagne, and still hadn't found Muriel. I smiled and made polite conversation with strangers and the few people I happened to know.

Somewhere between an autographed Seven Drift guitar and a vacation trip to Italy, Tucker cornered me. "Thinking of bidding?" he asked. He stood next to me, hands clasped behind his back, attention trained on the items in front of us.

"No. They're all a little out of my price range," I admitted. A sideways glance revealed that he was much taller than I'd realized, and he smelled phenomenal. Like soap and spring rain. I gave him a smile, hoping to ease the tension stretching between us. "You?"

He gave a noncommittal shrug. "I find that hard to believe. You being a millionaire and all." A hint of southern drawl teased his words.

I bristled, and my defensive walls snapped into place. "My financial situation is hardly any of your business." I wanted him to like me for Sam's sake, but I wasn't about to be a doormat for anyone. Not anymore.

"What's your angle anyway?" he asked. Our eyes met. His brimmed with blatant hostility tempered by genuine concern. My dismay lessened a bit. I couldn't blame him for being concerned about Sam. In fact, I respected him all the more for it.

"No angle."

The line had begun to move again. I stepped along with it, and Tucker followed at my elbow.

"I find that hard to believe, given your track record." He smiled at a young lady modeling a pair of leather driving gloves, handmade in Italy. She blushed and smiled back. While his voice and demeanor remained pleasant, his meaning was unmistakable.

"I appreciate your concern for Sam, but you've got nothing to worry about."

He leaned down until his lips paralleled my ear. "Name your price. Whatever it takes to get you out of his life."

My insides twisted. I bit my lower lip to hold back a verbal torrent of hurt and anger. It seemed I would never escape my error in judgment. I felt trapped in an infinite loop, destined to relive my betrayal over and over again. Perhaps this was my own version of hell.

"There is no price," I hissed through clenched teeth.

Tears burned my eyes. I blinked them back. I refused to let him see the way his words wounded me. And then I had a revelation. I would never be able to control what others thought of me. I could only control my reaction to their barbs. Something clicked inside me. The constriction of self-loathing eased the smallest bit. I was able to draw breath again.

"Girls like you always have a price." Tucker's eyes narrowed, burning into me.

"First of all, I'm not a girl," I said. "And second of all, does Sam know you're over here acting like his father?"

Tucker looked down at his feet, conflicting emotions flickering over his features.

"Listen. I get it." I touched his arm to show my sincerity. "You're worried about him, and you have every right to question my motives. I know my word doesn't mean much, but I promise you I'll never willingly hurt him again."

"I hope that's true," he said, blinking up to me. His eyes were hazel and rimmed with thick black lashes. Behind the questions and distrust, they were kind. "Because another deal like that might break him."

After the conversation with Tucker, I headed for the ladies room to regroup. I felt raw and unpeeled, like my skin had been stripped away and only my bare bones remained. On the way there, I took a wrong turn and found myself in an unfamiliar hallway. I was about to double back when a door opened in front of me. Jared MacGruder, Dahlia, and Malcolm Seaforth strode from the room. Taken aback, I stepped into an alcove, not wanting to interact with my three least favorite people.

I drew in a deep breath, leaned into the shadows, and counted to thirty. When I stepped out of my hiding place and into the light, I came face to face with Malcolm Seaforth.

Chapter 22

Sam

I WATCHED DAKOTA cross the dance floor and meander through the auction items. She stopped here and there to admire an item or chat with an acquaintance. I couldn't take my eyes off her, even when MacGruder said my name three times in a row. Tucker held fast to her elbow, giving her an earful, no doubt. I knew he questioned her motives. I also knew Dakota wouldn't take any of his shit. I thought about running interference but decided to let them work it out. Nonetheless, I breathed a sigh of relief when they parted ways and no blood had been shed.

The silver dress looked stunning on her. My imagination ran wild, wondering what she wore beneath it. Fantasies of the hem pushed up to her waist, long legs straddling mine in the limo, and those damned white panties from yesterday made my cock stiffen.

It had always been that way with us. I could never get enough of her. She turned me on in ways I'd never known possible. Time and betrayal hadn't lessened the attraction. If anything, my anger toward her only made me want her more. Like a dumb ass, I'd thought I could fuck her out of my head when all it had done was cement her there more firmly than ever.

I excused myself from MacGruder and pressed through the crowd toward her. I barely made it ten feet before someone touched my arm and pulled me into a conversation I didn't want about things that didn't matter. By the time I'd gotten to her side of the room, she'd disappeared into the back hall. I trailed along behind her, certain I'd catch her, eager for a few minutes alone. My father caught up to her first.

When his fingers wrapped around her arm, a fury unlike any I'd ever known turned my vision red. I blamed him for everything, for her betrayal, for my unhappiness. He'd stolen the most precious thing in my life from me, and before I drew my last breath in this world, I'd make sure he paid the price for it.

Dakota flinched away from his touch. To someone who didn't know her, she would have looked calm and prepossessed, but I recognized the sheer terror on her face. Her fear made the beast rage inside me. I curbed my temper and stepped into the shadows. They were less than a yard away from me, and I could hear every word they said with disturbing clarity. I should have interrupted, demanded he take his hands off her, but part of me wanted to see what she said. I guess I still didn't trust her, and this was the ultimate test.

"You're looking very pretty tonight." The coldness in his voice disturbed me more than his words. "Are you ready to renew our partnership yet? I've got some great new propositions for you." She ignored him and tried to push by, but he held on to her. He laughed. "Think very carefully before you answer, Dakota."

The expression on her face won me over. She lifted her chin, jutting it out in that stubborn way of hers, and squared her shoulders. An air of calm descended over her. "Let go of me." His hand dropped away, but his sadistic smirk remained. "Don't ever touch me again. Don't speak to me. And don't ever make the mistake of thinking I give a damn about what you think."

"Such a fireball. I admire that about you," he said. "If only I were twenty years younger, I'd give Sam a run for his money." My gut twisted with disgust when his gaze traveled over her. "Or if age isn't an issue for you, maybe we could work something out."

"You're revolting." Dakota took a step backward, bumping into a small table near the wall. Its contents wobbled. He followed her. In another few steps, my position would be exposed.

"I could use a wife. Think about it." He straightened his tie, eyes still locked onto Dakota. My Dakota. "You could have the use of my money, and I could have the use of you."

Hatred for Malcolm Seaforth swelled inside me. Father be damned. My fingers curled into fists, and my vision turned a murderous red. He'd gone too far. Just when I thought he'd reached the limit of vulgarity, he always surpassed my very low expectations. A few weeks ago, I would've been curious to hear Dakota's answer, but all I wanted to do now was rescue her from his villainous antics.

I must've made a noise, because my father looked up and smiled. He stepped back from Dakota and raised his hands in a gesture of peace. "Samuel. I was just telling your young lady how lovely she looks tonight."

"Are you ready to go, Dakota?" I asked, extending a hand toward her.

She slid her fingers through mine. I drew her to my side, wanting to protect her. Touching her soothed the urge to pummel his face. If I snapped, he'd claim it as a victory. Rising to his bait would only exacerbate the situation. He wanted a reaction from me, any reaction, and I refused to give it.

"Have you told her about our new corporation yet, Sam? Dakota will be interested in Seaforth and Seaforth. I'm sure we can find a place for her there."

His words followed us down the hallway. I felt her stiffen beside me. Her curious gaze weighted my shoulders.

"What's he talking about?" she asked.

"Nothing," I replied.

At the end of the hallway, she stopped. "Talk to me, Sam."

"There's nothing to talk about." I tried to tug her forward, but she planted her feet and refused to budge an inch. Always stubborn. Always persistent. Always questioning.

"You need to tell me what's going on. Right now." Her eyes darkened at my hesitation. "You still don't trust me."

The disappointment in her voice struck a nerve inside me. I had wanted this evening to be fun, not laden with the baggage of our past. I watched as my plans crumbled into dust, but I did nothing to stop the disintegration. "It's no big deal. The man's delusional. He thinks I'm going to join forces with him." *Stupid ass.* I mentally chastised myself. *Tell her. Tell her.*

"You mean he wants you to come to the dark side?" She lifted an eyebrow. Her ability to find humor in the bleakest situations only endeared her to me more. "And what did you say to that?"

"I told him not to hold his breath." I stared from the dark hall into the bright ballroom where the people milled about, oblivious to my turmoil. Gentle notes of classical music haunted the hallway. I wanted to tell Dakota more, about the special delivery packet, about his threats, but the words clogged in my throat. I was beginning to trust her, but I didn't have the balls to make the leap of faith. Once I lowered the barrier between us, I'd be a goner. I'd have to admit I was in love with her.

"What's it going to take?" she asked, reading my thoughts. "Do I need to bleed before you'll trust me?"

"It's not that simple."

"Really? Because it seems simple to me. Either you trust me or you don't."

I grabbed her hand again. "This isn't the time or the place for this conversation.

We can talk about it later."

She sagged against the wall. Her features drooped, and the hopelessness in her eyes tugged at my heart. "I'm exhausted, Sam. I'm constantly afraid I'm going to do or say the wrong thing. I feel like you're always judging me, waiting for me to screw up." I took a step toward her, wanting to comfort her, but she shook her head to ward me away. "The pressure is making me crazy."

"I'm sorry." I shoved a hand through my hair.

"So am I."

I raised her hand to my lips and placed a kiss on her knuckles. "This will be over soon. We'll talk then, okay?"

"Sure." The flatness of her tone frightened me. She pulled her hand from mine and straightened her shoulders. "I'm going to the ladies room. I'll catch you in a few minutes."

"Promise?"

She smiled, but it didn't reach her eyes. I felt her slipping away from me, withdrawing. Panic tightened my chest. I watched her walk along the corridor, afraid to take my gaze from her. I remembered how much it hurt to lose her, the devastation of our divorce bubbling to the surface of my memories once again. I was going to lose her altogether if I wasn't careful, and this time it would be no one's fault but my own.

Chapter 23

Dakota

I DRAGGED MY fingers through Sam's and left him at the entrance to the ballroom. His gaze weighed on my backside, but I didn't look back. The encounter with his father had left me cold, and I needed some time to pull myself together. I expected Malcolm Seaforth's manipulative antics. In this respect, he never disappointed. After the tete-a-tete with Tucker, Malcolm's antics seemed anticlimactic. But I hadn't expected Sam to shut me down with his distrust. I'd proven myself to him time after time, but his inconsistent behavior was beginning to wear away at my optimism for our future.

If I'd been less disturbed, I'd have paused to admire the damask wallpaper and muted gold color scheme of the ladies room. Floor-to-ceiling mirrors tracked my steps across the plush carpet. I'd only made it halfway into the room when I froze. Dahlia stood in front of one of the mirrors, hands braced against the marble counter, head down. She lifted her eyes to meet mine in the mirror's reflection, and

I saw streaks of tears down her cheeks. With a sniff, she straightened her shoulders and dabbed at her face with a tissue.

"Excuse me," I said, intending to pass her by.

"No, wait. I'm glad you're here," she said and turned to face me. She wore an exquisite black gown. Geometric cutouts exposed portions of her cleavage and tanned flat belly. I was pretty sure the girl had never eaten a donut in her life. "I've been wanting to talk to you."

"Sure," I said with a politeness I didn't feel. I had a few questions for her as well. The time had come to clear the air between us. "I've got a few questions for you, too."

"Fire away," she said.

"I saw you with Sam's dad." At my words, a flicker of panic sparked in her eyes. "Does Sam know you're talking to Malcolm?"

"We bumped into each other in the hallway," she said with a dismissive wave of her hand. "I was only being polite."

"I don't believe that for one minute."

"I know who you are. Sam told me."

These words stopped me in my tracks. "Told you what?" I held my breath, not wanting to hear what she might say, but knowing it need to be said anyway.

"That you're his ex." The tissue crumpled in her fist. "It all makes sense to me now."

A frisson of panic gripped my chest. I had the feeling she was about to reveal an unpleasant truth. "It's not a secret." I schooled my features into ambivalence and took a place beside her at the mirror. "It's a matter of public record."

"I wondered why he wanted you around when you're so obviously not right for Infinity, or him." Her pale blue eyes studied me. "And now I get it." I focused on my reflection and pretended to repair my makeup. "It's all about revenge and power for him. You're just another piece in his chess game, and he'll throw you away when he's done with you. Like he always does."

Knives of insecurity sliced through my fragile self-confidence. "I wonder what he'll say when I tell him you were talking to his father?" I tried to touch up my lipstick with a trembling hand.

She smiled. "Does it really matter? He won't believe you anyway. We both know he doesn't trust you out of his sight."

She'd put into words the very thoughts plaguing my subconscious for the last few weeks. I scrambled to hold my control in place, not wanting to give her any indication how her confession affected me. I tossed my lipstick into my clutch and turned to leave.

"I was there for him," she said to my back. "I put the pieces back together when he was broken. I saw how much he hated you for it. Don't make the mistake of thinking he cares for you."

My hand was on the door to leave, but something stopped me from escaping. The whole situation with Sam, his father, and Dahlia seemed so absurd it was laughable. I knew I should keep walking, ignore her diatribe, and get on with the evening, but I was tired of accusations and innuendoes. It would never stop unless I put an end to it. I turned to face her once more.

"Maybe you should follow your own advice," I said. "Don't make the mistake of thinking you know how he feels. Sam does what Sam wants, and you'd do well to remember it." Her face fell the tiniest bit, and I knew I'd struck a nerve. I could've devastated her with a few well-placed barbs, but I'd lost the taste for hatred and revenge. "And thank you, by the way."

"For what?" She stared at me in confusion.

"For taking care of him when he needed it," I said and shut the door behind me.

* * *

I didn't go back to Sam. Instead, I wandered toward the nearest exit, hoping for fresh air and a reprieve from the drama of the night. I found a small balcony off the ballroom and stepped outside. A warm wind carried the scent of roses from the garden. The swimming pool gleamed below me, its blue waters illuminated like a jewel in the night. I pressed a hand to my stomach, attempting to quell the butterflies of distress and drew in a deep breath.

I loved Sam. I knew this beyond question. I always had and I always would. But I needed more than a one-sided affair. I needed to know he loved me, too. In spite of all the mistakes I'd made, the many ways I'd betrayed him, and my utter failure at being a wife, I realized I was only human. I deserved another chance at love and happiness.

With a sinking heart, I had to admit Sam might not be the one for the job. If he couldn't get over the past and learn to trust me, we had no hope for a future together. Tears burned my eyes and throat. I needed some kind of sign that we were making progress in our relationship. The constant back and forth was draining away my self-esteem. And when it was gone, I'd have nothing left.

"There you are." Sam's greeting caressed my ears as he pressed against my back. "I've been looking everywhere for you."

"I needed air." His arm slid around my waist, drawing me closer to him, exciting all of my nerve endings, the way it did every time he touched me.

"Everything okay?" The brush of his lips across the top of my head renewed the sting of tears behind my eyelids.

"No, it's not." I tried to pull away from him, although every fiber of my being yearned to burrow deeper into his embrace. His arms tightened around me until I could feel his ribs against my back and the thickness between his legs nudging my bottom.

"What's wrong? Let me make it right." The way his deep voice rumbled in the quiet night air did crazy things to my heart.

"I saw Dahlia with your father and Jared MacGruder tonight." I was in no mood to skirt around the issue. Better to rip the bandage off in one sharp tug than to prolong the agony. "Right before you came into the hall. They were all together."

"Really?" He swayed gently in time to the music wafting through the open balcony doors. "That's weird."

"It was weird. And when I asked her about it, she wouldn't answer me."

"Are you sure? I can't believe she'd do something like that." I stiffened in his arms, but he didn't seem to notice. "Maybe you took things out of context."

I pushed away and turned to face him, my heart hammering in my chest so loudly I could scarcely hear my own voice. Because this was it. This was the moment where he either believed me or he didn't, trusted me or not. "No. I know what I saw."

He reached for me, but I hovered out of range, knowing the moment he touched me again, I'd cave. I'd give in to lust and longing and forget all my principles.

"She wouldn't do anything like that," he said, frowning.

My heart plummeted into the abyss of disappointment. "So you don't believe me?" I tried again.

"Of course I believe you. I just don't believe Dahlia would betray me. We've been friends forever. I trust her."

And there it was. The truth. Laid out nice and pretty in front of me with a big, fat bow on top. He took a step toward me, but I backed up, my heart breaking into a million pieces. Moonlight glinted off the waves in his messy hair and sculpted the bones in his face. He'd never looked more irresistible, more beautiful, or more unattainable.

"But you don't trust me." I shook my head, blinking away the blur of tears. "You're never going to trust me. I get that now."

"Kota, come on." He blocked my escape with a side step. "Be reasonable. We both agreed we needed time."

"No. You needed time." I pressed a hand to my stomach, hoping the crab cakes and oysters from our dinner would remain there. "And I thought I could give it to you, but...I can't do it."

"What do you mean, you can't?" The fear in his voice renewed the surge of anguish inside me.

"You make me doubt myself." I gave up the pretense of control and let the tears flow down my face. "You make me think I'm a horrible person when I'm not. I'm just a girl who made a mistake--a huge mistake--one I learned from."

"Wait." Sam's full lips pressed into a tight line. "You're not a horrible person, Dakota."

"It's okay, Sam." I drew in a shuddering breath and plunged onward. "I don't blame you for it. I just can't live like this, having to prove myself to you over and over."

"What do you expect, Dakota? You left me." The words burst out of him with a fury I hadn't prepared for. I blinked. "I keep wondering when you're going to leave again. Will it be today? Tomorrow? Next week?"

"That's not fair." His anger knocked the wind from me. "You know why I left. It's not like that now."

"Really? It's not?" He shoved a hand through his hair, jaw tightening. "Isn't that what this is? You leaving me? Again?"

Shock, anger, and disappointment silenced us both for the space of a dozen heartbeats. We stared at each other, the emotional distance widening between us with every passing second. I saw it all on his face--betrayal, resignation, and accusation. Even now, I still loved him, and I couldn't bear to see it end like this.

"I'll finish out the MacGruder project," I said, straightening my shoulders.

"I appreciate that," Sam replied, his tone cold.

"We can still be friends." I choked on the words, wanting to throw myself into his arms and beg for him to love me instead.

"We were never friends," Sam said. And with those words, he turned and walked away.

Chapter 24

Dakota

I APPROACHED MONDAY morning with the enthusiasm of a woman about to face the firing squad. On the drive to work, Rockwell had to stop the car twice so I could heave the contents of my stomach onto the roadside. When he finally parked in front of the office steps, I remained in the car, too anxious to move.

"I just need a minute," I said. His sympathetic gaze met mine in the rearview mirror.

"Take as long as you want," he replied and offered a handkerchief from the breast pocket of his shirt.

With a grateful nod, I took it and withdrew a compact mirror from my purse. I wiped away smudges of mascara beneath my eyes and tried to regain my composure. I refused to let my personal issues take precedence over my professional obligations. Sam and I were parting as adults this time, under mutual consent, but it was still difficult.

When I was twenty, I'd ended my marriage to Sam under threats of blackmail and harm to my family. I'd been devastated. At the charity auction, I'd ended our relationship to preserve my self-esteem. Once again, I found myself heartbroken. This time, however, was different. This time I knew I could survive. The knowledge didn't lessen the pain. Now that I'd had a taste of Sam, I wanted him in my life. A solitary tear leaked from the corner of my right eye. I swiped it away.

"May I say something?" Rockwell interrupted my breakdown. I glanced up to find his face etched with concern.

"Of course," I said.

"It's not over until it's over." He twisted around in the seat to face me. "As long as the sun comes up in the morning and you both have a heartbeat, it isn't finished."

"Easy for you to say." My lower lip trembled with the threat of another tear. "You didn't see the way he looked at me. I'm pretty sure we're through for good."

"You guys have been through hell. He loves you. And I know you love him back." I nodded. His reached a hand over the back of the seat to cover mine. The reassuring warmth buoyed my strength. "He's scared, Dakota. Scared you'll leave again. Can you blame him?"

"I know," I whispered. "But I can't be with him when he doesn't believe in me." My defenses bristled at the need to once again explain myself. "And I haven't left. I'm still here. When I leave this time, it will because he made me go." I worried the hem of the handkerchief between my fingers. The silk threads of an embroidered bluebird adorned one of the corners. I stroked the tiny stitches, relieved by the distraction. "My mother has a hankie like this."

"I know. She gave it to me." The smile on Rockwell's face lit up the interior of the car. Happiness rushed through me to see the raw emotion in his expression. He was such a good man, kind, patient, and loyal. I was going to miss him. The thought brought a resurgence of tears to my eyes.

"Rockwell, are you seeing my mother?" A crimson tide rushed up his neck and into his cheeks. He'd been a positive influence in Sam's life, and I appreciated his support through the past tumultuous months. My mother deserved a man like Rockwell.

"She's a good woman," he said. "Like you."

"Thanks." His praise meant more to me than I cared to admit.

Rockwell's fingers tightened around mine. "Now get in there and show our boy you mean business."

Xavier met me at the beverage station. He poured coffee into my outstretched cup then watched as I emptied two packets of salt into the black liquid. I realized my mistake, sighed, and dumped the coffee into the sink.

"That bad?" he asked. He shook his head and refilled my cup along with two more.

"Yes." As soon as I spoke, Sam appeared at Xavier's elbow. The bottom dropped from my belly at the sight of his straight nose, square jaw, and high cheekbones. Smudges of exhaustion darkened his eyes, but he managed a polite smile. I longed to caress his cheek and wipe away the lines of worry on his forehead. Bittersweet emotions twisted inside me. A flutter of excitement preceded the pang of heartbreak. I tightened my fingers around the cup handle and stared into its dark contents.

"Good morning." The rich timbre of his voice shimmered over me, awakening the ache between my legs. If my body responded to him in this way every time he spoke, it was going to be a very long day.

"Morning," I replied and watched him take the cup from Xavier's hands, unable to meet his gaze. My attention focused on his adept fingers, the ones so skilled at arousing me.

"I've asked Mark to meet with me at ten," Sam said. I blinked up at him then away. It was like looking into the midday sun, bright, hot, and unyielding. Sam stared at an undisclosed point above my head. "I'd like you to join us."

"Okay." And then he was gone. I resisted the urge to follow him with my gaze as he walked away and concentrated on stirring my coffee until it splashed onto the counter.

"Brrr." Xavier shivered and searched my face with curious eyes. "Someone's in the doghouse."

I didn't reply and turned toward my office instead, harried thoughts whirring inside my head. Xavier's footsteps tapped on the wood floor behind me. Why couldn't he just mind his own business? I was in no mood for his games this morning.

"I know your secret, by the way," he offered when I moved to shut the door between us. "Mrs. Seaforth?"

This caught my attention. I froze mid-step. He pursed his lips. We stared at each other for several seconds before I took him by the arm and pulled him into my office.

"Who told you?" I asked, shutting the door firmly behind us.

"Dahlia." Xavier's face brightened. "She's devastated by the way. Congratulations."

"Your empathy is overwhelming." I slid into the chair behind my desk and powered on the computer. Xavier leaned against the wall beside me, gripping his coffee cup in both hands.

"Don't feel too sorry for her. She's more interested in Sam's social status than his heart." He rifled through the sheaf of papers at my elbow until I placed my hand on top of it. "Which belongs to you from what I've seen."

"I'd rather not discuss it," I said.

"I have a whole new respect for you. That man is a handful on his best day. I can't imagine what it was like to be married to him. Let alone divorced and working together." Xavier continued, undisturbed by my rebuff.

"It hasn't been a picnic, I can tell you that," I muttered and punched my password into the keyboard with short, angry pecks.

An overwhelming sense of exhaustion sapped the strength from my body. I leaned my head against the back of the chair and closed my eyes. I was so tired of the lies, the charades, and the constant strain of dancing around the situation. I no longer had the fortitude to pretend I didn't care.

"Lucky for you, this job is almost over, right?"

"Right." Panic intensified the tired ache. In a few days, this torture would conclude. Sam would close the MacGruder deal, and I would move on. Tears stung my eyes. No more head games. No more angry sex. No more Sam. The finality of the situation settled over me, weighting me down.

"You never struck me as a quitter." Xavier nudged the vase of roses, which always sat on the corner of my desk, toward me. "Fresh white roses every day. For you. From him. It was a very specific request."

My attention returned to the crystal vase and the twelve stems tipped with ivory blossoms. I'd assumed they were part of the office décor, replenished by housekeeping. They were my favorite and always had been. Back when we were married, Sam had given me a flower every day. Sometimes it was a dandelion, sometimes a rose, but it was always there beside my breakfast plate or on the bed pillow in the morning.

"I take care of all his personal appointments, you know," Xavier continued. He stroked the closed petals of a bud. "Since you arrived on the scene, not one afterhours meeting." He drew air quotes around *afterhours* with his fingers. "No weekend hotel reservations. No secret luncheon dates. And he asked me to give a canned rejection to any calls from his lady friends."

At the mention of the other women in Sam's life, the hair on my arms bristled. Even though my fears regarding Fran had been allayed, I had no illusions regarding the future. Once I left the picture, Sam would be back on the market, and there would be plenty of women waiting to take my place.

"I'm sure he'll be back on the scene again." I kept my attention focused on the computer monitor while I choked down the bile in my throat.

"My wife and I are going out Saturday night. Why don't you come with us?" He took one of the flowers and plucked the bud from the stem before tucking it into the lapel of his lavender jacket.

Xavier had a wife? I had expected a male lover or lovers, but not a woman. In spite of my misery, I paused to reflect on this latest revelation. He smiled serenely at my thinly veiled surprise.

"Xandra," he said. "Also with an X. She's hot. Oriental. She will love you."

"Thanks, but I don't think so." By now my computer had come to life, and I focused on opening my email. The idea of sitting in a club ranked next to the firing squad. Until I could corral my depression, I would be spending my evenings at home with a pint of ice cream and a stack of steamy romance novels.

"I'm serious." Xavier stood and adjusted the knot of his electric blue tie. "You can't sit at home moping." He tapped a finger on the top of my hand. "And believe me, Sammy will have kittens when he finds out you're moving on without him. The guy hates to lose. Especially when it's something he cares about."

"I doubt that." I slumped further into my chair.

"Well, think about it. We go to Dystopia every Saturday night. You've got a standing invitation to join us." He turned and strode to the door with his peculiar, slinking gait. "And for the record? I'm Team Dakota all the way."

Chapter 25

Sam

ONE WEEK DRAGGED into the next. I'd thought ten years apart from Dakota had been torture. A decade of separation was nothing compared to seeing her every day, knowing I couldn't touch her, knowing we were over. Every accidental brush of our shoulders sent my pulse into overdrive. Each meeting of our eyes made my groin tighten with need. I could ignore the physical aspects of my attraction, but I hadn't anticipated the empty ache it fostered.

I missed her. Not the sex, although it had been epic. I missed the way her eyes lit up when she saw me. The flirty flutter of her lashes when our gazes collided across the conference room table. The way she bit her bottom lip when she contemplated kissing me. The secret way her little finger crooked around mine when we rode the elevator with a carload of employees. Even though we were over, she hadn't left me. She was still here, fulfilling her obligations, showing her loyalty to me when I deserved none of it.

I was standing outside my office when she approached from the elevators, Xavier at her elbow and a takeout box in her hand. Several more employees followed. Their laughter stopped, smiles replaced by frowns. I frowned back. Her eyes met mine, and my heart kicked against my ribs until I thought they would crack. I wracked my brain for something to say, desperate for interaction with her. "Have you got that report ready yet?" I asked.

"Yes." Her voice, devoid of warmth, bristled with professionalism. "Would you like me to email it, or do you want to go over it together?"

"Email is fine," I replied. The thought of sitting next to her, alone in my office, made my palms sweat.

"Okay," she said.

"Okay," I echoed, feeling more awkward than I had since puberty.

She turned and went back to her office. I stepped behind my door and closed it, feeling a hundred different kinds of wrung out by our encounter.

This agony was no one's fault but my own. I scrubbed a hand over my face, reminded by the stubble against my palm that I'd once again forgotten to shave. Shit like that didn't seem to matter anymore. What mattered was the love of my life sitting in an office two doors down the hall. Because she *was* the love of my life. The one. The only. No other woman would ever replace her. She'd stolen my heart and now held it captive.

Tell her. Tell her. Tell her. The words cycled through my head on a loop. *Get your ass out of this chair, Seaforth. Walk down the hall and tell her.* Something held me back. I was reminded of the envelope in my desk drawer containing all her secrets. I should give it to her, tell her about the meeting with my father, and let her choose what to do with the contents.

"Mr. Seaforth? Mr. Tucker is on line three for you," Mrs. Cantrell announced through the intercom.

I jerked, drawn out of my reverie by her thin voice.

"Fucker," Tuck said by way of greeting when I picked up the call.

I felt a modicum of relief at the sound of his voice. "You're the fucker," I replied. The threads of my sanity began to fortify. Tuck would bring me back to earth. He'd always been able to talk sense into me like no one else.

"That I am," he said, his lazy voice filled with amusement.

The tension eased between my shoulders. "Did you call for a reason or did you just miss the sound of my voice?" I kicked back in my chair, happy for the distraction.

"I called to remind you we're having drinks after work tonight. Mike's Martini Bar by the airport."

"Right." I'd forgotten, but some time away with my guys sounded like just the medicine I needed.

The moment I hung up the phone, a knock sounded on the door. Dahlia poked her head through the opening and smiled. I stifled a groan but motioned her inside with a wave of my hand. The hits kept rolling.

"Got a sec?" she asked. The easy tone of her voice raised my guard.

"Yes. Have a seat. I wanted to talk to you anyway." I clasped my hands on the desk and waited for her to ease into the chair across from me.

"Sure. You first." She crossed her legs. Her hands trembled as she smoothed back her hair.

"No. Ladies first."

She drew in a deep breath before speaking, as if fortifying her courage. "It's about Dakota."

"I don't want to talk about Dakota."

"She's a distraction. She's throwing you off your game." She leaned forward, features drawn in concern. "I'm worried about you, Sam."

"I'm fine, Dahlia." Was it so obvious? I studied her eyes, the dark eyeliner surrounding their perimeter, and the hedge of thick lashes. Faint lines of age webbed the corners of her eyes.

"I remember how you were before. I just don't want to see you that way again."

Dahlia and I had a lot of history. She'd helped me out of more than a few unhappy situations, and she'd always been there when I needed her. I liked and respected her. And I'd known her long enough to recognize the impending argument looming on our horizon.

"You don't know anything about it." I'd told her about the divorce years ago, but I'd never gone into the sordid details.

"I know enough, Sam." She uncrossed her legs and placed a hand over mine. "Your father told me how she played you from the start, the poor girl chasing after the rich guy. What she did to you is inexcusable."

"You talked to my father?" Heat climbed my torso and ignited my blood. Unable to contain my anger, I sprang to my feet and paced the length of the office. "What the fuck, Dahlia?"

"It's not like that." A frown flitted across her face.

"You know how I feel about my dad." I shoved a hand through my hair to keep from exploding in a fit of temper. "You talked with him behind my back?"

"Calm down, Sam. He asked to meet with me. He's concerned about you." She rose from her chair to stand beside me. Her hand rested on my arm to calm me, but all it did was fuel my wrath. "I'm concerned."

My laughter echoed through the office. "That's the funniest thing I've heard in a long time. My dad doesn't give a shit about me, and you know it." I shook off her hand. "How much did he pay you to spy on me?" Her face fell along with the bottom of my stomach. I knew with that one gesture Dakota had been right about her. I opened the office door. "Get your shit and get out. We're done."

* * *

Mike's Martini Bar did a good business in spite of its south side location. The tiny building could fit inside the bathroom of my Chicago penthouse. The floors were uneven and the food questionable, but the martinis were the best in the city. Mike served us himself. He was a middle-aged retired Army sergeant with a crew cut and a beer gut, but he had a knack with gin and vermouth that had landed him on the pages of several magazines and one television show.

"Thanks, Mike," I said as he delivered a tray of chilled goodness to our table. I pointed to Tuck. "You can give him the bill."

"That's right. Put it on my tab, Mike," Tucker said, stretching lazily as he spoke. "Now that I'm a gazillionaire, I can afford to help out my freeloading friends."

Tucker was a millionaire several times over by birth. His father had invented one of those crazy gadgets advertised on late-night TV, the thing everyone had to have but no one ever needed. As a result, his family's wealth exceeded my own. And like me, Tucker had chosen to make it on his own, creating video games, subsisting on popcorn and potato chips, socking every spare penny into his work. To date, he'd garnered nothing but a few freelance jobs for the big gamers.

"You mean you finally sold one of those sorry things?" Beckett asked. He'd come to Mike's straight from the office and always exuded primal energy afterward, like a rubber band stretched too tight and about to snap.

"Not only did I sell one of those sorry things," Tuck replied, drawing out the answer with dramatic flare, "but I also sold the entire series. All of it. For an exorbitant amount of money."

"No shit?" I took a sip of my martini and let the complementary flavors of gin, vermouth, olive, and onion sizzle across my tongue. Warmth spread through my chest, and the tension of the day eased from my muscles.

"No shit." Tuck looked pleased, his eyes bright with pride. "Big bucks, my friends."

"How exorbitant?" Becks asked, squinting in disbelief. "Like, Donald Trump exorbitant? Or hey-let-me-get-this-round-of-drinks exorbitant?"

"Well, maybe not Donald Trump exorbitant, but enough to live on for the next forty years or so." He grinned modestly. "Face it, boys. I'm a success."

We raised our glasses in a toast to Tucker. I clapped him on the back, knowing how hard he'd worked and all the doubt he'd garnered along the way. His parents treated his career like a joke, and I had to admit, I had also. This put me in my place, lending perspective to how arrogant and narrow-minded I'd become.

"That's great, man," I said. "You deserve it."

"So what are you going to do with all that money?" Becks asked.

"I don't know. Take a vacation maybe. I hear the surfing is great in Australia." His gaze rested on mine. "What do you suggest, Seaforth? You're the money whiz."

His words snapped the reality of my financial situation to the forefront of my thoughts. The trust in his gaze twisted my guts. I forced a bravado I didn't feel. "Invest. Diversify. Depends on your long-range goals."

"Don't have any yet," Tuck said, his interest focused somewhere over my shoulder. I shifted to follow the trajectory of his attention. Three long-legged beauties had just entered the bar. "But I think my short-term goal just walked through the door."

"Nice." Beckett nodded, taking in the women with appreciation. They were flight attendant types, the kind who frequented this bar between layovers, drawn by the nearby airport and hotels.

"You in?" Tuck asked with a nod toward the women.

"Nah. I've got work to finish tonight." All the talk about money reminded me of my priorities. None of them included getting laid by a stranger.

"Such discipline," Beckett said.

"He must be getting it somewhere else," Tucker added, searching my face with more acuity than I cared for. "Speaking of which, you owe me a thousand dollars, fucker."

"For what?" I asked.

The three women smiled at us, their gazes roving from Tucker to Beckett and finally resting on me. The game had begun. One I didn't intend on playing. I turned away from the girls and trained my attention on the soccer game on the flat-screen TV near us.

"For the Charity Auction? You were supposed to bring a date, remember?" Tucker replied.

"I had a date." The words stuck in my throat as memories of that night danced through my head. I still found it too painful to think about, but hell if I'd let them see it.

"Your ex-wife doesn't count," Beckett interjected. He smiled and nodded to the girls behind me. "I want the redhead."

"You always get the redheads." Tucker scowled. "Maybe I want the redhead this time."

"Guys." I rolled my eyes and tossed a twenty on the table to cover my bill. Before I could rise from my stool, I smelled sweet perfume and felt the heat of someone standing behind me.

"Hello, gentlemen." The redhead spoke in a low, husky voice, the kind promising fun and heady sex. "Can we join you?"

"Please." Tucker gestured to the empty seats next to us, while Beckett pulled a stool to his side.

"Here. You can have my seat," I said, standing.

"Leaving so soon?" The question came from a slender brunette at the redhead's elbow. She was tall with big tits and a tiny waist. "I was hoping to get to know you."

Her large brown doe eyes drank me in. For a nanosecond, I contemplated my options. After all, I was a free man. Dakota and I were over. I could take this girl home, shag her rotten, and never speak to her again. I waited for the pull of lust, the familiar tightening in my groin, the surge of animal need, but it never came. It never arrived, because I wasn't that guy anymore. Three months ago, I'd have been all in, leading the pack, vying with them for the prettiest girl. But today, I wasn't the one who fucked anonymous girls in dark corners or had sex for the sake of getting off. I was the guy whose heart belonged to another woman. One woman. And her name was Dakota.

Chapter 26

Sam

A FEW MINUTES past midnight, the strain of digesting reports and figures finally got to me. I removed my reading glasses and passed a hand over my eyes. No matter how may times I read through the data, the numbers didn't change. The balance of my accounts continued to dwindle with each passing day. Although I acted as CEO for Infinity, I had a dozen smaller companies, personal holdings, operating under different names in different locations across the country. I used these businesses to hide from my father, to make acquisitions and inquiries, stealing deals from beneath him. Every extra nickel of my personal salary went back into funding my vendetta.

I'd been so focused on my revenge that I'd failed to take into account the hundreds of lives affected by my plan. I'd done a terrible thing, something I'd regret the rest of my life. As they always did, my thoughts drifted to Dakota. Once, she'd done a terrible thing, too. It was within my power to forgive her, and I hadn't done it. Given my current situation, I was in no place to judge her. Weariness seeped into my bones. I felt older than my thirty years, weighted down by anger and responsibility. I hadn't realized the burden those emotions put upon me. I thought about my friends, out enjoying the summer night, the way I should be, and how disappointed they would be to hear of my failure.

I kicked back in the chair, my gaze falling on a sweater Dakota had forgotten after one of our meetings. I retrieved it from the chair where she'd dropped it and lifted it to my nose before taking a long, deep breath. It smelled like her, fresh and clean, her floral perfume mingling with a hint of fabric softener. Even if our romantic involvement had ended, we were connected by our past. We could be friends, and friends talked on the phone. Before drawing my next breath, I'd convinced myself.

I went for my phone and dialed her number. A thrill of anticipation gave purpose to my actions. She was probably in bed. The image of her curled on her side, face pillowed in one of her delicate hands, sheets clinging to her curves, revved my flagging spirits. On the sixth ring, she finally answered.

"Yes?" she shouted into the receiver, her words distorted by blaring music in the background.

"Hey," I said, trying to hold back the twitter of excitement at the sound of her sultry voice. "What are you doing?"

"Hanging with some friends," she replied. Hoots of laughter floated over the music. "Why? Is something wrong?"

"No." I felt a pang of unreasonable irritation to find her out and about. I'd assumed she'd be at home, tucked into the safety of her apartment. I'd drawn upon the notion often over the course of the evening, finding comfort in the idea, but Dakota never did what I expected. Of course, she had a life outside of Infinity, one that didn't include me. What healthy, single, attractive girl spent Friday nights at home alone? The realization realigned my expectations in a most unpleasant way.

"Are you still at work?" she asked. By the slight lilt in her speech, I knew she was tipsy.

"Yes." I frowned at the computer screen and the ugly secrets it held. "Finishing up some things."

"Poor Sammy. All work and no play." Her breathy teasing stole my focus. Sober Dakota was enticing, but an inebriated Dakota held a magical power all her own. The last time I'd seen her drunk, we'd been twenty years old. She'd been at a girlfriend's bachelorette party all night. When she got home, she hadn't been able to keep her hands off me. We'd had sex underneath the kitchen table, on the sofa, and in the closet. It was damn near the highlight of my sexual history. That night would be forever emblazoned on my memory. The way her nails had dug into my ass as I'd pounded into her. Her tiny grunts and moans of ecstasy. The tightening of her thighs around my waist as she'd come.

"You aren't driving, are you?"

"Nope. Are you?" she asked then giggled.

A masculine voice interrupted our conversation, low and deep, like he was close to her ear. The hairs on the back of my neck lifted in proprietary dismay.

"Hey, got to go. Catch you later."

"Wait, I--" She hung up before I could finish. Knots of unease tightened in my gut. Who the hell was that guy? I had a vision of Dakota in one of her sweet little dresses, surrounded by horny Neanderthals eager to get their hands on her. With a growl of frustration, I paced a few rounds of the office before calling her back. The call went straight to voice mail after a dozen rings.

"What's up?" She answered the next call on the fifth ring this time, sounding as if I'd interrupted her. Uncertainty made me hesitate. I felt like an awkward teenager with a crush, stalking the babysitter. "This had better be important."

"We got disconnected. Where are you?" I asked.

"Hmm...don't know." More laughter. More music. My fingers tightened around the phone while I waited for her reply. "Where are we?" she asked someone. The man's voice replied, and it sounded like she cupped a hand over the receiver for a second. "Uh, Dystopia."

"Who is that guy?" I knew Dystopia, an ultra-swank club with VIP rooms and velvet ropes and bouncers dressed in three-piece suits. It was the place where guys like me, Tucker, and Becks went to pick up women. A small fire lit in my veins.

"Eric." Her flirtatious tone knotted my gut. "Say hello, Eric."

"Hello, Eric," he said.

Dakota erupted into fits of laughter.

I'd never considered myself a violent man, but right then and there my attitude shifted. Breath whooshed out of my lungs, hissing like steam from a teakettle. I didn't know Eric--hell, he was probably a nice guy--but if we'd been face to face, I would've been pleased to introduce my fist to his face.

"Are you on a date?" I asked, then gritted my teeth while she took her sweet time answering.

"Wouldn't you like to know?" Her flirty tone did crazy things to my lower half. Fuck if I didn't want to reach through the phone and snatch her to me, hold her tight, and never let her go. "But no. I'm flying solo tonight."

"I'll be there in twenty minutes," I said, already through the door, car keys in hand. She might not want me there, but I wasn't about to give her to another man without checking him out first.

Once I arrived at Dystopia, it took another twenty minutes to locate Dakota. I found her in the back, crammed into a dimly lit booth with Muriel and two other men. They were clean-cut and handsome. I pegged them as investment bankers.

The guy beside Dakota had his arm draped over the backrest behind her, his fingers hovering millimeters from her shoulder, a clear territorial marker. I stared at him through narrowed eyes. He grinned up at me, oblivious to who I was and why I was there.

I nodded to Muriel. She lifted a hand in a halfhearted wave, dislike clouding her features. I never came face to face with the victims of my acquisitions. Muriel was a casualty of one of those deals. By the coolness of her gaze, she hadn't recovered. Guilt warred with the other emotions in my head. I had become *that* guy--the one who valued money over people and success over happiness. If I needed proof, I found it in Muriel's cool reception.

"Hi," Dakota said, smiling up at me. Even in the dim light, I could see the aquamarine of her irises, made brighter by the hue of her blue dress. It was low-cut, showing the upper swells of her breasts, and just as sweet as I'd imagined. "You remember Muriel? And this is her friend, Vance."

"Hello, Muriel. Nice to meet you, Vance," I said, but I couldn't tear my gaze from Dakota's. Something new and unsettling swirled in her vibrant eyes.

"And this is Eric."

A subtle shift of power blossomed between us. In the boardroom, I ruled everyone and everything, but outside the office, not so much. Definitely not with her. I thought I was in control of my feelings, of our relationship, but the guy sitting next to her suggested otherwise. For the first time, I realized--if I wasn't careful--I could be replaced. My shoulders tensed.

"Hey, Sam." The guy lifted his chin in greeting. "Good to meet you."

"Hey." I didn't like him, not one bit. Not his clean-shaven face. Not his short, neat hair. Not his pale blue polo shirt, nor the burgeoning smirk on his lips.

"Pull up a chair, Sam." His fingers grazed the top of Dakota's shoulder.

I narrowed my eyes. His hand swept across her fair skin to curl around her bicep. A pulse of white-hot male proprietary anger shot through my veins. He was touching my girl. My girl. Mine.

"Let me get you a beer." He motioned to the waitress. An investment banker, handsome, and he was nice. Fan-fucking-tastic.

"Thanks, but I'm just here to get my wife. We really need to get going. Are you ready, Dakota?" I asked.

"Wife? I had no idea." Eric lifted his hands in the air, palms facing toward me. "She didn't say anything about being married."

"Because we're not," she said. "He's my ex-husband." By the tone of her voice, she was more amused than annoyed.

"Come on. Let's go." I held out a hand and gestured for her to take it.

"He's very bossy," she told the table at large but didn't budge an inch.

"That's because I'm your boss," I replied. "That's what bosses do. They boss people."

She lifted her beer to take a sip, staring at me from over the brown bottle with large, round, mischievous eyes. "In case you didn't notice, I'm off work. I'll be back at the office around seven on Monday."

"We have some pressing business for you to take care of," I said, forcing an even, quiet tone. Our gazes locked in a battle of wit and will.

"As you can see, I'm busy right now. Why don't you leave me a voice mail? Or better yet, send an email. I'll take a look at it as soon as I'm free." Full, pink lips pressed against the mouth of a long-necked beer. Lips capable of taking me to heights of pleasure or tearing me to shreds with a single word.

Eric glanced between us. "Maybe you should step off, fellow," he said. "It sounds like she doesn't want you here." I could tell by his halfhearted tone that he was making a gallant gesture, secretly hoping one or both of us would leave. He clearly had no interest in confrontation. I met his kind all the time in the conference room. I ate men like him for breakfast.

"Do you want me to leave?" I asked Dakota.

Someone cleared his throat behind me. I turned to see Xavier hovering at my elbow, Xandra at his side. Xavier's wife always made me uncomfortable. She consistently stood too close, touching my arm or chest when she talked, smiling a little too brightly. At all the company functions, I went out of my way to keep a wide personal space between us.

"Hello, Sam," Xavier said. "Are you going to join us? Can I get you a drink?"

"I'm not staying."

They brushed past and crowded into the booth with the others. Six pairs of eyes stared at me. Muriel and her date seemed nervous, exchanging glances and frowns. Xandra's focus roved from my head to my toes a little too enthusiastically, making me grateful for the layers of dress shirt, suit jacket, and trousers between us. Xavier studied me with expectant calm, like he was waiting for me to snap, enjoying every minute of my discomfort.

Eric shifted away from Dakota, obviously uncomfortable beneath my caveman stare. "Is there going to be a problem?" he asked. "Because I'm just out for some fun tonight. I've got my own ex to deal with. I don't need tangled up in someone else's marital issues."

Dakota's laugh sent a flush of heat into my cheeks. "No problem," she said. "I was ready to go home anyway." She slid out of the booth and stood, wobbling on her stiletto heels. "Thanks for inviting me out, Xavier."

So the little peckerhead was responsible for this. His eyes met mine then flicked away. I could only guess what he was up to. He smiled at Dakota, lips curving up like quotation marks, genuine affection in his expression. "Thank you for coming. It's been a pleasure."

The dimples on either side of Dakota's mouth deepened with her smile. "Nice to meet you, Xandra. And you too, Eric." He nodded, relief obvious on his face. "I'll call you later, Muriel."

"Tomorrow," Muriel said with another significant glance at her date. "Not too early."

"You got it." Dakota straightened and drew in a breath, fortifying herself. Even on those rare occasions when she'd been drunk, she always kept it together. She did so now, smoothing her dress over her hips and thighs, before turning to look me in the eye...and walking right past me.

"Wait up," I said and lurched after her. The crowd of people surged and ebbed around us. For a fraction of a second, I lost sight of her amid the sea of strangers. She seemed determined to lose me. When she reappeared a few feet in front of me, I grabbed her elbow. "Hang on, Atwell."

"You've got a lot of nerve showing up here." She faced me, lips pursed. A drunk bobbed past us and knocked Dakota into me. Her breasts flattened against my chest, soft and warm. I placed a hand on the small of her back, holding her there, prolonging the effect.

"I wanted to make sure you got home okay," I said, staring into her upturned face, enjoying the way it felt to have her pressed against me.

"You wanted to make sure I got home without Eric." One of her brows arched in reproach, but her eyes continued to twinkle with merciless merriment. "For the record, Seaforth, you've got no right."

"I know." Seeing her with Eric had made it painfully obvious. For the briefest of moments, I tumbled into the ebony pools of her pupils, dilated in the darkness.

She placed a hand on my chest and pushed away. "Don't forget it." She looked so delicate and strong at the same time. When she lifted her chin in defiance, every muscle in my groin tightened. I loved the fire in her eyes, the way she never backed down, even when she was in the wrong. "You can take me home now."

"Okay."

Her hair was down the way I liked it, tumbling in loose waves over her breasts, brushing my hand as she moved away. Once again, she was on the move, surging toward the exit. The music swelled, making more words impossible.

When I'd seen Eric's arm around Dakota, I'd forgotten about everything else. All I could see was his hands on my girl, my wife, my love. Mine. The solitary word kept pulsing through my head over and over. Mine. Mine. Mine. After the million ways she'd broken my heart, I still wanted her all to myself. She still belonged to me.

Ahead of me, she pushed through the exit door and onto the sidewalk, pausing at the curb. I signaled to the valet for my car. Dakota and I stood in silence. She listed to one side, similar to a young tree during a strong wind. Fearing she might topple off her tall shoes, I reached out to steady her, but she waved my hand away. The warning in her eyes disrupted my calm. I'd breached her personal boundaries by showing up here, and she had every right to be pissed. Palms sweating, heart skipping, I stared straight ahead, feeling the same way I had in the principal's office during grade school.

"And another thing..." She also stared across the street. "If you ever do something like this again, I will have your balls for breakfast. Do you understand?"

"Why are you always disrespecting my balls?" God, how I loved her smart mouth. I licked my lips and fought away a smile.

"Because you're a caveman." I heard the hint of amusement return to her voice. "And it's the only way I can get your attention."

Chapter 27

Sam

FIVE MINUTES INTO the drive home, Dakota fell asleep in the passenger seat of my car. Her head lolled from side to side as I turned into the service drive of Infinity. When I put the car in park, she mumbled and roused enough to protest. I ignored her mutterings and struggled to extract her from the car. She'd somehow managed to tangle her arms and dress in the seat belt.

"I said you could take me home. My home. Not yours." She fumbled with the seat belt release, cursing beneath her breath.

"My place was closer."

"I call bullshit." She yanked on the seatbelt again, her frustration mounting as her motor skills deteriorated.

"You're getting drunker," I mused. "How can that be?"

"I had a couple of shots right before you got there. They seem to be hitting me." Amused by her confession, she giggled. "Right now."

"You're going to feel like shit in the morning. You know that, right?"

"Do you have pizza?" she asked, eyes widening. She tugged on the seat belt again. "Don't just stand there. Get me out of this thing."

"Hold your horses, sweet pea." I rolled my eyes, secretly amused.

I leaned into the car and tried not to look down her top at the smooth swells of her breasts. She relaxed into the seat with childlike resignation and waited while I untangled the restraint. After a few false starts, we strode down the curved walk to the back door. It had been a servants' entrance once, leading to a narrow corridor and the stairs to my suite of rooms in the back of the house.

At the stoop, I balanced Dakota on the top step with one hand while I searched my pockets with the other. Too late, I realized I'd dropped my keys somewhere along the way. I propped her against the doorframe.

"You smell nice," she said, leaning toward me to sniff my neck and almost falling face first into the darkness. I caught her and leaned her back against the house. "You always smell like sin."

"Sin?" I chuckled, checking my pockets for the elusive key once more. "I didn't know sin had a scent."

"It does, and it smells like you." She smoothed a hand over the placket of my shirt. The muscles of my groin tightened at her touch. Our eyes met. I recognized that look, the heat of desire building up behind her irises, the way her gaze dropped to my mouth. "You make me want to sin. A lot."

"Stay here a second," I commanded in my sternest voice. "I'm going to go find the keys. Can you do that?"

"Sure." The way her lower lip curved into a smile drew my focus. "See you later."

"I'm coming back, goofy girl. Don't move."

I turned and trotted down the walk, using the flashlight app on my phone to search the area. A glint of silver winked from the ground next to my car. I sighed in relief, shoved the keys into my pocket, and jogged back to the house. The stoop was empty, Dakota gone.

"Kota?" I groaned and scanned the darkness, wishing the landscape lights stayed on past midnight.

"Over here." A small hand shot up from the forsythia bush a few yards away.

"What the hell?" She was lying on her back amid the leafy brambles. "What are you doing?" I hoisted her out and attempted to brush away bits of bark and leaves from her dress. My hand grazed her breast. I jerked, embarrassed by the accidental contact. I stumbled backward, tripping over a sprinkler head in the process. She snorted with laughter. As if on cue, a fine mist of water shot from the irrigation system, dousing us both. A dozen more sprinkler heads popped up. Water hissed through the air, plopping onto the grass. I wrapped an arm around her waist and half-dragged, half-carried her through the spray and into the house.

"I didn't see that coming," she said. Inside the laundry room, water puddled at our feet. The wet fabric of her dress clung to her curves, and the damp locks of her hair were plastered to her head. I could only guess my appearance was similar. "You look ridiculous."

A rivulet of water ran down my forehead. I swiped at it and glowered at her. My ruined silk shirt was plastered against my torso. I plucked it away from my skin. It gave way with a suctioning noise. "This is your fault. Why can't you ever do what I ask?" I grumbled as I searched the linen closet for towels. "Just once. Is that so much to ask?"

"I like yanking your chain," she said on an exhaled breath. "And you make it so easy."

"Well, you've become an expert at it." I grabbed two fluffy towels and tossed one at her. It hit her in the stomach and fell to the floor. She stared at her feet, swaying.

"It's a long way down there," she said after a few seconds of contemplation.

Her eyes met mine, warming my insides like a shot of whiskey. "I might not make it back up."

A smile lifted the corners of my mouth. I shook my head, retrieved the towel, and began rubbing the wetness from her skin. I started with her shoulders, sweeping down the toned length of biceps to her fingers then across the expanse of her chest. I lingered over the tops of her breasts, enjoying the intake of her breath as I did so.

"Go ahead. Take it off." I nodded to her dress.

"No." She scowled at me.

"Your teeth are chattering so loud I can hardly hear myself think." The defiance in her gaze made my pulse leap. So obstinate, my little Dakota. I used my thumb to brush a drop of water from her cheek.

"This is a ploy to get me naked, isn't it? Well, it's not going to work this time." She crossed her arms over her chest. "You and your sexy abs and your mouth." Her gaze homed in on my lips. "Why do you have to be so gorgeous? Why can't you have a Quasimodo hump or something?"

I lifted an eyebrow, flattered and irritated in equal measure. When I tried to unzip her dress, she flinched like I'd stung her.

"No." Fire danced in her eyes.

"Jesus. Are we really going to argue about this?" As usual, she knew exactly how to push my buttons. "Take off the freaking dress, Kota."

"I said no." When she tried to step away, her foot slipped in the water. She fell back against the washing machine, hands floundering wildly in the air for purchase.

I grabbed her by the biceps, steadying her until she stabilized. She was rigid as an iron pipe in my grasp. "Baby, please." The tension eased in her muscles. Feeling the smallest modicum of surrender, I continued in my best persuasive whisper. "You're drunk and soaking wet. Let's get you into something dry and warm before you catch cold. All right?"

"Okay." Her gaze softened. "Will you fix me a peanut butter sandwich? I'm starving."

"Yes." I tapped the tip of her nose with the towel. "Anything you want, darling."

Chapter 28

Sam

AN HOUR LATER, we sat in companionable silence before the fireplace in my living room. Dakota wore one of my T-shirts. The snowy white cotton skimmed over her curves and bare legs. I found it difficult to concentrate on anything besides the tension in my groin, knowing she was naked underneath. She clasped her peanut butter sandwich in both hands. I didn't know how to cook many things, but I'd perfected the grilled peanut butter sandwich during our marriage. She'd remembered, and it touched me.

"Mm...so good," she mumbled through a mouthful. When her tongue swept over her lower lip, I had to suppress a groan.

We'd done this so many times before the divorce. She would curl up on the couch with a book, while I sat a few feet away at the kitchen table to study. Those were the happiest times of my life. Things had been simpler then. All we'd needed was each other. The sight of her now, on my sofa with one bare foot tucked beneath her, hair spiraling over her shoulders, affected me in ways I hadn't known possible. It seemed so right to have her there, natural even. I swallowed against the thickness forming in my throat.

"You want another one?" I asked.

"No." She popped the last bite into her mouth then snuggled into my shoulder.

Without thinking about the embargo on our relationship, I wrapped an arm around her and pulled her close. Her head rested in the crook of my neck like it belonged there. Because it did, I realized. I shut my eyes, savoring the scent of her shampoo, the heat of her body through the thin cotton of the shirt. Sitting in that way, it was easy to pretend we were still together, that we'd never been apart.

I dropped a kiss onto the top of her head. "I've missed this, baby. Have you?"

A soft snore greeted my question. With a forefinger, I swept the hair from her face. Dark lashes fanned over her cheeks. I traced the slope of her pert nose. Her lips curved into a smile. I pressed a light kiss there, not wanting to wake her.

Once I'd extinguished the fire, I carried her to my bed and tucked her in. I wanted to wake her, tell her how much I loved her then show her with my lips and hands. Instead, I sat in the chair across from her and watched her sleep, realizing I'd missed my opportunity to make things work between us. The truth twisted inside me. We were over, but I wasn't ready to call it quits.

"Sam?" Her soft voice floated through the night air. "Come to bed."

It was an invitation I only needed to hear once. I pulled my shirt over my head before lying on the bed beside her. Stretched out on our sides, my front to her back, I wrapped an arm around her waist and pulled her tight to me. She sighed and nestled her bottom into the curve of my pelvis. We weren't together. I had no idea if we ever would be. But at this moment, holding her in my arms was the closest to heaven I'd ever been.

Chapter 29

Dakota

THE NEXT MORNING, I awoke in Sam's bed, but he was nowhere in sight. Hazy snippets of the previous evening teased my memories. The effort to think sent white-hot pokers of pain shooting through my temples. I gripped my forehead and eased from the bed before padding barefoot down the hallway. I found Sam in the kitchen, reading the newspaper with a cup of coffee in his hand. He was wearing boxers and a white cotton T-shirt, blond hair rumpled, bare feet resting on the rungs of the barstool. The scene was heartbreakingly familiar. My throat tightened with longing and regret at the sight of him. When he saw me, a wary expression guarded his eyes.

"Coffee?" I croaked through a dry throat.

"Espresso." He cocked an eyebrow, knowing how that one word would affect me, and gestured toward the steaming cup on the breakfast bar across from him.

I gripped the mug with both hands and took a sip before humming approval.

"Oh, God, I love you," I murmured then froze in panic. Did I really just go there? "I mean, thanks."

He laughed, but his eyes remained somber. "No problem."

"Please tell me I didn't humiliate myself." As I slid onto a stool, I caught sight of my reflection in the stainless steel toaster. My hair stood on end in a rat's nest of curls. Mascara smudged beneath my eyes. I covered my face with a hand, mortified. "Shit," I mumbled, unable to meet his gaze.

"It's okay," he said and ever so gently pulled my hand away from my face. His eyes brimmed with amusement. "You look beautiful to me, Kota."

Heat rushed from my toes to the tips of my ears. I lowered my gaze to the countertop. "I'm so embarrassed."

"Maybe it wasn't your proudest moment," he replied, "but you did fine."

We sat across from each other, avoiding eye contact. Minutes ticked by with painful slowness. I swallowed the two aspirin he'd left beside my coffee cup and tried to regain my composure.

"Well, this is awkward," I said when the silence became unbearable. I had no idea what to say or how to make sense of the situation.

"Pretty much." He set his cup on the saucer and slowly lifted his eyes to mine. With his hair mussed, fresh from sleep, he looked like my Sam, young and breathtaking. One corner of his mouth curled up in a reluctant grin. I couldn't help smiling back. And then we were laughing, shyly at first, then full-bellied guffaws.

When I was able to catch my breath, I wiped tears of amusement from my eyes. "I fell in a bush."

"You did," he said, green eyes twinkling.

"And we got wet." I snorted.

"We did." He pushed a lock of hair from my face. My pulse pounded in my temples. A little flutter started low in my belly. "Because you never listen."

"No." I wasn't sure whether to laugh more or cry. All of my cells cried out for him. A biological response completely outside of my control.

"I miss you," we said in unison.

"What are we going to do?" I asked, overcome by the bittersweet sensations of lust, longing, and love. "You said we weren't friends, but you're my best friend, Sam. I can't be around you and not want to be with you."

"Then be with me," he said. In one smooth motion, he slid from his stool onto his bended knee. His fingers found mine. I stared into his eyes, soft with sincerity. Familiar warmth started from my chest and suffused my body. There was nothing more tantalizing than a big guy on one knee in front of a girl.

"Nothing has changed," I said. "You don't trust me."

He stared at our clasped hands. His thumb brushed over my knuckles, back and forth. After a lengthy exhale, he said, "I trust you. You've more than proven yourself to me." His brow furrowed. "You with that guy made me crazy." The timbre of his voice lowered. "I didn't like it."

"You're having a knee-jerk reaction to seeing me with someone else," I said. "It's normal."

"You're my wife," he said, his grip tightening on my hand. "Seeing you with someone else will never be normal for me."

I wanted to believe him with every fiber in my being, I found it hard to believe he'd worked through his trust issues overnight. We'd been at odds for the better part of the last two months. As much as I loved him, I wasn't going to leap into his arms and pretend everything was okay. Not until I was sure. Not until I knew this wasn't going to end badly.

"We've really fucked this up, haven't we?" Tears of regret pricked my eyes. I blinked them back, focusing on our clasped hands.

"Don't say that." He lifted our hands and pressed a kiss to my fingertips.

"Where do we go from here? We can't be together and we can't stay apart." I blew out a tremulous breath to lessen the painful squeezing of my heart.

"Would it make a difference if I said I love you?"

His words jerked my attention to his face. There he was. My Sam. The guy who loved me. The depth of emotion in his gaze rocked me to the core. For the first time in weeks, I had hope for us. For more.

"It does." I placed a finger on his lips to stop him from speaking. "But not yet. Not like this."

He nodded and nipped my finger with his teeth. "I get it. We'll take our time, baby girl." He rose to his feet and stared down at me, long and lean and muscular. The cocky grin on his mouth revitalized my hopes. "But just so you know, I'm in it to win it."

Chapter 30

Sam

THE NEXT WEEK passed, the same as the one before it. There were meetings and conference calls and a trip to Chicago sandwiched into the middle. I put my home office up for sale and made arrangements to liquidate as many assets as I could manage. The cars, the houses, the boat--none of those things held meaning for me. They were merely markers of wealth, status symbols in a game I no longer cared to play. In a few days, I'd call a meeting of the board members to discuss the state of the corporation. They needed to hear the news from me and not someone else.

When the weekend came, we celebrated Mrs. Atwell's birthday at Rockwell's house. It was just me, Dakota, her mother, and Rockwell lounging by his pool on a hot July afternoon. I sat on Rockwell's deck, watching Dakota from behind my mirrored aviator shades as she floated on a raft, admiring the fit of her blue-and-white bikini and wondering how long until I could get her alone and take it off.

Rockwell sat beside me, shirtless, beer in hand, tanned and toned. We did this often when the weather permitted, just the two of us, sitting in deck chairs next to the pool, sometimes talking and often times not. He had a nice place. I paid him well and from the looks of things, he'd invested his money wisely. I was relieved to know he'd be fine in spite of my mistake. Over the years, he'd been more of a father to me than Malcolm Seaforth ever was. Rockwell was the one who'd taught me how to throw a baseball; he'd attended every game and school event I'd entered, had stood by my side through the black days after my divorce, and never doubted me even at my worst.

"You ever been married, Rockwell?" I asked after a long silence.

"No," he said. With his sunglasses on, I couldn't see where he was looking, but I suspected his gaze was locked on Mrs. Atwell. She sat on the edge of the pool, legs dangling in the water, chatting with her daughter. She was still a good-looking woman. The women seemed comfortable. In fact, the whole scenario seemed too good to be true.

I had to wonder if this is how things would've been with us if we'd stayed married. Would we have had a house in the suburbs, a pool, her mother visiting on the weekends and Rockwell hanging out after work? A sweet pang of longing sliced through me. I didn't need the fancy cars or the big houses. I just needed this. Her. Us.

"Why not?" I picked up the thread of conversation after a few minutes.

He lifted a shoulder and dropped it. "I don't know. There was someone once, but she was married and way out of my league." He took a drink of his beer, swallowed, and tapped a finger on the bottle before continuing. "I guess time got away from me and next thing you know, I'm old and she's dead."

"It was my mom, wasn't it?" I already knew the answer. Even as a kid, I'd seen the way he'd looked at my mom. I felt a pang of regret for him, knowing he'd never had what I had with Dakota. I watched her paddle around the perimeter of the deep end, splash water on her mother, and laugh. I could never get enough of that sound, her laughter. It filled all the cracks and spaces inside me, and made me whole again.

"Yeah." He leaned forward, elbows on his thighs, clasping his beer bottle in both hands. "She was a lot different when she was young. Pretty thing. Your father didn't treat her very well. She was going to leave him, but then you came along. Then your sister. Your dad threatened to take you both away, declare her unfit if she left. He's a powerful man, your dad, and he could do it. She was too scared to go."

"Did she know?" I couldn't face him, so I kept watching Dakota, pleased by her smile when she glanced my way. The scent of chlorine hung in the air tempered by the heavy sweetness of the honeysuckle vines entwining the privacy fence.

"I never told her. Hell, I had nothing to offer someone like her. I just stood on the sidelines and watched her die inside, one day at a time." The deck chair creaked as he leaned back. "She'd be proud of you, son. Her kids were always the light in her life."

"Thanks." I coughed to cover up the emotion welling inside me and looked away.

"So what's going on with you two?" He pointed his beer at Dakota. "You back together or what?"

"I don't know. Maybe." I'd been asking myself the same question for days. "For now, I guess."

"She loves you something fierce," he said. "And if you ask me, she always did."

"Well, I didn't ask you," I replied.

"Never stopped me from giving you my opinion before." His deep chuckle brought a reluctant grin to my face. "Won't stop me from giving it now either."

Dakota rolled off the raft and dog paddled to the shallow end where we were sitting. She bobbed in the water, droplets of water shining like diamonds on her tan, creamy skin. Her long, brown curls looked black when they were wet. "Are you coming in or not?" she asked. When I shook my head, she splashed water on me. "Afraid you'll mess up your hair, pretty boy?"

"Do that again and I'll take you across my knee," I said, hoping she'd take the bait. Another splash of cold water rewarded me, soaking my board shorts. I set my beer on the deck, tossed my shades into the grass, and dove into the pool after her. She squealed and tried to swim away, but I caught her by the ankle and dragged her back to me. No matter how hard she tried to get away, I couldn't let her go, would never let her go.

Chapter 31

Sam

ON THURSDAY OF the following week, I called a meeting of the private shareholders and board members of Infinity Enterprises. Tucker, Beckett, Rockwell and my sister Venetia, who'd flown in reluctantly from Las Vegas, were all in attendance. I invited Dakota as well. If we were going to make a go of things, she needed to know where I stood financially--which was, frankly, in the toilet.

"What's she doing here?" Venetia asked when Dakota entered the room.

Venetia was a smaller, feminine version of me. Tucker had dated her once but had said every time he'd gone to kiss her, he'd seen me, and it was just too weird. Thank God for small favors, because I would've beaten his ass the first time he'd stepped out on her.

"I agree," Beckett said. "She shouldn't be a part of this."

Dakota's cheeks turned bright red. I shook my head when she tried to stand up. "They're right," she said. "I'm not a part of this. I'll go."

"Stay." I rested my hands on her shoulders and gently pushed her back into the chair. "You need to hear what I've got to say."

Her gaze flicked from Tucker to Venetia and back to me, a crease between her brows.

"I don't want her here," Venetia said. "I don't trust her."

Dakota twisted in her chair, discomfort obvious. I stroked the back of my hand over her cheek, and she smiled at me. Always brave. Always a fighter. My chest swelled with love for this indomitable woman.

"Neither do I," added Beckett.

"I do," Rockwell interjected. I shot him a grateful glance for always having my back. "I trust them both."

"You know I'd trust you with my life, Sammy," Tucker said. "If you want her here then I'm good with it."

"How do you know she's not going to run back to your dad with whatever goes down here today?" Beckett asked.

Dakota's face fell. Tension clogged the air. I felt her unease as if it were my own. It was a fair question. How did I know? I stared at her, rifling through the bits and pieces of our shared past. Once she knew I was broke, would she leave? I still wasn't completely certain, but at some point, I had to take a leap of faith. In my heart, I had no doubts. It was my head that couldn't agree.

"She'll stay for the first part," I said, raising a hand to quell their murmured dissent. "And then we'll conduct the rest in private."

Chapter 32

Dakota

I LISTENED IN shock as Sam began to detail the financial status of the company. Property values had plummeted over the past month due to overseas wars and instability in our country's government. Basically, he was at a fork in the road. He could continue with the MacGruder acquisition, putting the future of Infinity at financial risk, or he could shelve the entire deal. He'd already taken steps to liquidate his personal assets and offset the debts with cash from his pockets. Either way, Infinity was in trouble, and it would take a miracle to save it.

When he finished, everyone sat in stunned silence. I bit my lower lip, uncertain if I should leave at this point, but wanted to stay and offer comfort to Sam. He stood at the head of the table, tall and strong, ready to bear the blame. I knew without asking what had happened. He'd been playing a very dangerous game of chess with his father, countering Malcolm's moves with his own, blocking the man into a corner. The burden of responsibility rested squarely on my shoulders. I'd driven him to this, ruined him by loving him, and sealed the deal by returning to his life.

"If you'll excuse me," I said, rising from my chair. The room grew smaller with each passing moment until I could barely draw breath. I needed to get out.

The door closed behind me. I sprinted down the hall in search of fresh air. Sam caught up with me at his office door. He opened it and tugged me inside. I stared up at him, palm to my chest, waiting for my blood pressure to level out.

"What are you thinking?" he asked. Green eyes searched mine with equal measure of desperation and resignation, as if he already knew the answer and dreaded to hear it.

I waited a few seconds before speaking, choosing my words carefully. "You did this because of me." I clenched my hands into fists at my sides, unable to look at him. "You put your money and your friends' money in jeopardy over some stupid vendetta."

"I want him to pay for meddling in our lives, for making us miserable, my mother, Venetia. I thought it would make up for ruining your life." The remorse in his voice caused me to step back. My heart broke again, hearing his anguish.

"He hasn't ruined my life yet," I said. "I'm here in spite of him. We're together in spite of what he did."

"Every day without you was hell for me, Dakota," he said, his voice cracking with emotion.

"It was hell for me, too." I took his hand and pressed the back of it to my cheek. "But I took the check. Me. I could've walked away. I didn't. I take full responsibility. You were right to hate me, because this whole deal is my fault."

"He backed you into a corner. You felt like you didn't have a choice." With a sudden yank, he pulled me into his arms, squeezing me so tightly I thought my ribs might crack. The beat of his heart thudded beneath my ear. He radiated heat, burning through my clothes and searing my skin.

"I had a choice, Sam." I felt safe wrapped in his arms, even if it was only temporary. "I made the wrong one, but it was my decision. Just like you're making the wrong decision now. You need to understand that. Put the blame where it belongs."

"I've lost everything," he said into my neck. "It's too late."

"You haven't lost me, Sam. I'm still here." My voice began to grow in loudness, buoyed by my frustration and his hardheadedness. "Screw the money. I don't give a damn if you're rich or poor. It was never about the money," I shouted, not caring who heard me.

He pulled away from me, staring at me like I'd lost my mind. "You'd stay? Even if I lost everything?"

"Don't do this. If you make the MacGruder deal to ruin your father then you'll be just like him. And I'm telling you now, I don't want to be with that kind of person." The confusion in his eyes got to me, tore me up inside, and made me want to cry for putting it there.

"We need to talk this through." He stood up straighter, squaring his shoulders. "Wait here, would you? I need to finish this meeting and then we can talk it out."

I nodded and watched him leave, uneasy about the shift in dynamic between us. To calm my nerves, I paced around his office, studying the artwork and the framed diplomas near the door. He had a bachelor's degree in architecture and a master's in business. There were various awards and certificates there as well. Pride filled me. He'd done well, my Sam.

An hour passed. I sat in the big leather chair behind his desk, touched all of his desk accessories, and sent text messages to my mother and Muriel. After awhile, I grew bored and decided to make a grocery list. I rifled through the top drawer of his desk for a notepad and pen. And that was when I saw it. A plain manila envelope with my name on it.

I shut the drawer and tried to pretend it wasn't there. I made a list of all the things I needed to restock my refrigerator: milk, eggs, cereal, and a dozen other items. Finally, I gave in and withdrew the envelope. I would just take a peek. It had my name on it, after all.

I undid the clasp and drew out a stack of papers. A dossier of everything I'd done over the past ten years spilled onto the desk. A sheet of paper outlined each of my former employers, along with detailed salary information, former places of residence, and financial data. This disturbed me on a number of levels, but it was the photographs that made me sick to my stomach. Photos of my college graduation. Grainy snapshots of me at bars and clubs. A second sheet of paper listed every guy I'd ever dated, their addresses and occupations. The business card paper-clipped to the top bore the name of a local detective agency.

Sam had been following me for years. He was still having me followed. The last report was dated a few weeks ago and had pictures of a shopping expedition with my mother, eating dinner at a Chinese restaurant, and walking along the street afterward.

In a daze, I put the papers back in the folder and fastened the clasp. I returned it to the top drawer and closed it. My actions were slow and controlled, but my thoughts whirled through my head in a chaotic mess. He'd asked about where I'd been and what I'd done during those ten years, but he'd known all along. I wasn't sure whether to be flattered or horrified by his invasion into my privacy.

I drew in a deep breath and tried to sort my emotions. As the shock abated, hurt replaced it. Why hadn't he told me about this? For the past two months, I'd been fighting to prove I'd changed, to prove he could trust me. Consumed by the battle, I'd overlooked one very essential fact. He'd changed. We'd both become very different people. I was willing to overlook his arrogance, his bossiness, and his need to challenge me at every turn. No matter how much I cared for him, I couldn't be with a man who didn't respect or trust me.

Our entire relationship had been a tangled mess of pretty, filthy lies. Some of them his. Some his father's. Some mine. I needed time to think, to sort the truths from the deceptions, and I couldn't do it there. Before I could talk myself out of it or make excuses for Sam's behavior, I gathered my things and left.

Chapter 33

Sam

IT TOOK TWO hours to sort things out with the board, but in the end, we came up with a solution that satisfied everyone. I resigned as CEO. Beckett would take over until they could decide whether to reorganize or dissolve. I walked out of the conference room lighter and happier than I had in ten years. As I returned to my office, I pulled the necktie from my shirt and unbuttoned my collar.

Dakota was right. I didn't need to ruin my father. Eventually, he would ruin himself. He'd end up alone with his piles of money and no one to share it with. If I continued the head games, I would end up just like him. By removing myself from the playing field, he held no power over me.

Somewhere along the way, I'd lost myself, lost sight of the man I wanted to be and the things that made life worth living. Like Dakota. She was the beacon of light at the end of a tunnel filled with darkness. I wanted to be a better man for her. From the first day we'd met, she saw only the good in me when no one else cared to look. It was the reason I'd fallen in love with her on a warm spring day during our senior year of high school. It was the reason I'd married her, and the reason I'd ask her to marry me again when the time was right. Because I did love her. I'd always loved her and always would.

I opened the door to my office, eager to start living the rest of my life with her, only to find the room empty. Xavier entered behind me, arms full of documents and files for me to sign.

"Have you seen, Ms. Atwell?" I asked, fighting back the distress swelling inside me.

"Yes. I saw her get in a taxi about twenty minutes ago," he said and dropped the files onto the table beside my desk.

"Did she say where she was going?" I scanned the desk for a note. Finding nothing, I checked my phone for a voice mail or text.

"No. Not a word." Xavier frowned, immaculate brows drawing together over his slim nose. "Would you like Mrs. Cantrell to get her on the phone?"

And then I saw it. The corner of the manila envelope sticking out of my desk drawer, the drawer I usually kept locked, the one with my father's blackmail folder inside it.

Chapter 34

Dakota

A TAXI MET me on the front steps of Infinity. The weight of the day descended once I settled into the back seat of the cab. Sam didn't trust me. I saw the truth with painful clarity. Nothing I ever did would rebuild his trust. There would always be some doubt in the back of his mind, and it would always come between us. Not that it mattered any more. I sure as hell didn't trust him. I was in love with the Sam of my past, not the vindictive, mistrustful man he'd become.

Tears burned my eyes and throat. I held them back, not only for the cabbie's sake, but for my own. Once I let them loose, they might never shut off.

The driver dropped me at the curb of my apartment. I trudged upstairs, too tired to think any longer, eager for a hot shower followed by a long nap and a glass of wine. The door of my apartment door was unlocked and slightly ajar. Fear jumbled the last of my common sense. Someone had broken into my place. What if the person remained in there? In all the murder mysteries I'd ever seen on TV, the victim ventured into their burgled home to find the culprit inside. My luck had been in a downward spiral all day. I decided not to chance it, called 9-1-1, and waited in the downstairs lobby instead.

The police arrived within thirty minutes. For the next hour, I had to list all the missing items: TV, microwave, laptop, tablet, some jewelry, small kitchen appliances, and a wad of cash I'd kept hidden in a jar in the bathroom. For the hour following, I had to recount all the people who had access to my apartment as well anyone who'd been there in the previous weeks.

"The lock on your door isn't broken," the officer said. "Whoever did this had a key."

"No one has a key but me," I said. "I just had the locks changed two weeks ago." I'd been too busy to give my mother the spare. It was tucked in the top drawer of my desk. Or was it? I didn't want to look, entrenched firmly in denial of the obvious culprit. Blood pounded through my temples. I placed a hand on my chest, unable to draw a full breath, filled with anguish.

"What about boyfriends or relatives?" The officer was a kindly man who reminded me of my late father, barrel-chested and world-weary. I shook my head. He pressed on. "Usually, when I see this kind of thing, it's someone you trust. We've already checked with the manager. He hasn't let anyone in."

I knew in my head it was Crockett, but my heart denied it. "No. There's no one."

Meanwhile, my phone buzzed with a plethora of incoming calls and texts from Sam. I silenced the ringer and finally shoved the phone into a drawer. He was the least of my worries for now.

The police had only been gone a few minutes when someone pounded on my door.

Sam stood in the hall, dressed in a green Henley with the sleeves pushed up over his forearms and dark blue jeans, looking more handsome than should be legal. He had a leather messenger bag slung over his shoulder. One hand raked through his hair, lines of concern etched on his face. When he saw me, his shoulders sagged, and he exhaled loudly.

"Are you okay?" he asked. His gaze roamed over me, desperate for reassurance. "I saw the police down the hall, and I freaked out." He stepped toward me, as if intending to pull me into his embrace.

I stepped out of his reach and shook my head. If he touched me, I would melt and forget all the reasons I was angry with him. "I'm fine. Someone broke in." I waved a hand toward the wreckage of the living room.

"Thank God you're okay," he said. "Do they know who it was? How did they get in?"

"I don't know." Under normal circumstances, I would've poured out all my suspicions about Crockett, but the information lodged in my head and refused to come out. Sam was a stranger. I'd been married to him, made love to him, and shared the most intimate parts of my life with him, but I no longer knew or trusted the man he'd become.

"Why didn't you call me?" He took a step toward the door.

I put a hand on his chest, gentle but firm, and kept him at bay. "I don't think so." My chest constricted, collapsing in on itself, caused by the vacuum where my heart had been. In this moment, with my apartment ransacked by my brother and my ex-husband on my threshold, I'd never felt more betrayed or more devastated.

Chapter 35

Sam

OVER THE YEARS, I'd learned to read people well. Dakota had always been something of an open book. She never tried to hide her feelings. All I had to do was look into her aquamarine eyes. What I saw there made my palms sweat and my fingers curl into fists. Or should I say, it was what I didn't see that unnerved me.

"I can't deal with you right now," she said. Her flat, unfamiliar voice chilled me to the bone. "I'm tired and it's been a long day."

She stared into the hall past my shoulder. I watched her with a growing sense of panic. If she shut the door, I might never get another chance to explain. Working things out seemed more important than anything else in my fucked-up life.

"You can't stay here." I dropped the messenger bag on a chair and planted myself in the middle of the room. "What if they come back?"

By the widening of her eyes, she hadn't thought of that. She wrapped her arms around her waist. I could sense the possibilities shuffling through her mind. "No. It's okay. They got what they wanted." She glanced away again. Her face was pale, her figure small, delicate. I wanted to take her into my arms, stroke her hair, and make all her problems go away.

"I insist." I pushed past her, enjoying her small snort of irritation. "Look, if you won't leave, then I'll stay. We can order in a pizza, and I'll sleep on the couch."

The door slammed behind me. "You can't just barge in here, Sam. What part of no do you not understand?"

"Pretty much all of it." I righted the overturned coffee table and took a seat on the sofa. "What kind of pizza do you want?"

A low growl erupted from the girl. She closed her eyes, and I knew from previous experience that she was counting to ten. When she opened her eyes, they simmered with hurt and frustration. "I saw the file, Sam," she said, her voice low and shaking. "It made me sick. All this time you've been watching me. That's something your father would do."

"Here." I pulled the manila envelope from my messenger bag and handed it to her. "It was delivered to my office a few weeks ago. A present from my dad. I never looked at it." She didn't take it, so I let it drop onto the coffee table. "You can keep it."

"Why should I believe you?" With her arms crossed over her chest and eyes narrowed, she'd never been more beautiful to me. This girl I could handle. As long as she was mad at me, she still cared.

"Because I've never lied to you."

"You said you'd take care of Harmony and you didn't."

"Jesus. Are we back to that again?" I sank further into the cushions and curbed the urge to swear. "Business is business, Kota. Get over it."

"Apparently, you aren't very good at it." She sank into the chair across from me, nose tilted into the air.

"You did not just go there."

We glared at each other for the space of a few heartbeats. She infuriated me, exasperated me, and thrilled me in equal measure. Even when we were angry at each other, it felt right to me. I loved to fight with her because it made making up so much better.

"What are you going to do about MacGruder?" she asked.

"I called him on the way over here. We tabled the deal for now." I waited for her reaction, uncertain which direction her thoughts might take. I decided to plunge headlong into the unknown. I'd come this far. There was no reason to stop now. "And I resigned as CEO from Infinity. I'm done."

"Oh." Her lips formed a perfect circle with the word. Blood thundered in my ears while I waited for her to process what I'd said. She rubbed her palms on her thighs like she was nervous. "So what are you going to do now?"

"I don't know." I shrugged and reached across the breach between us to grab her hand. "I thought you might be able to help me figure it out."

Chapter 36

Dakota

THAT NIGHT WE ate too much pizza and fell asleep on the couch. I had to admit, it felt right to have him there. In the morning, with swatches of sunlight pouring into the apartment, Sam helped me clean up the disorder of the previous day. We didn't talk about the future or our relationship. We just moved from moment to moment, clinging to the fragile threads that held us together.

I didn't know what to make of the current state of our affairs. He seemed sincere about the dossier, and my gut said I could believe him. My heart had already forgiven him. It was my head that couldn't wrap around the situation.

Our relationship was so unconventional. It defied all the rules. We fell in love. We married. We divorced. Where did that leave us now? How did someone rebuild a relationship that was so utterly broken?

"What's this for?" Sam held up a rubber chicken key chain, silver key winking in the light.

"It's my spare key," I said and took it from him. "Where did you find it?"

"It fell out of your desk drawer. Is that where it goes?"

I couldn't answer. Tears of relief spilled over my cheeks. I sank onto the nearest chair and pillowed my face in my hands.

"Baby, what's wrong?" Sam kneeled in front of me and tried to pull my hands away from my face.

I shook my head, embarrassed by the outburst and unable to stop it. "I thought it was Crockett," I said when I could catch my breath. I folded my hands in my lap and stared at them as a new and unsettling thought occurred. "I suppose it could still be him. Maybe he had a copy made. Or he could've put it back before he left. I can't even trust my own brother."

Sam brushed the tears away with his fingers. "It wasn't Crockett."

"He's done this kind of thing before." Anger and frustration tensed the muscles in my forehead. I felt a headache coming on. "I'm so stupid. When will I ever learn that I can't trust him?"

"Kota, look at me." He covered my hands with his, warm and familiar. "It wasn't Crockett."

"You don't know that." His green eyes held mine as I rambled. "He's been getting worse and worse. Always lying. I don't know what to do with him anymore."

"Crockett's in rehab. The center called me yesterday to update his status. He couldn't have done it."

"Why would they call you?" He didn't answer, but he didn't have to. Rehab centers didn't take charity cases. Someone must have paid Crockett's fee. I knew without asking that it had been Sam. Even in the wake of his financial crisis, he had found the money to help me.

Our eyes met. I cupped his cheek, savoring the familiar scratch of stubble against my palm. He turned his face into my hand and placed a kiss in the center.

"Why?" I asked, my voice cracking over the single syllable.

"Because I knew it would make you happy," he said.

Chapter 37

Dakota

A WEEK LATER, the red Porsche rounded the street corner and raced in my direction. Whether I was eighteen or thirty, the sight of Sam's blond hair blowing in the wind always affected me in the same way. My breath came short and my heart kicked against my ribs. I raised a hand to pull the clip from my hair to let it tumble down my back, knowing he liked it that way.

He parked at the curb in front of me and swung the door open. "Get in," he said, his voice low and commanding.

"You're late," I replied as I slid into the bucket seat.

"And you're a pain in my ass," he said, "but I like you anyway."

We shared a smile. His eyes fell to my lips. He leaned in, the smell of his cologne spicy and sweet. My heart lurched. Our mouths hovered a millimeter apart, savoring the anticipation of meeting. When he kissed me, the taste of peppermint tingled on my tongue.

"I've been standing on the street for a half hour," I said the instant we parted. His lips were red with my lipstick, slightly swollen, and moist.

"Jesus, woman. Give me a break, would you?" With a rev of the engine, the car leaped into the street. He shot a sideways glance in my direction, green eyes assessing. "You said the corner of Fifty-Third and Belmont. This is Fifty-Third and Belleview."

"No. I did not." I frowned, replaying our earlier conversation in my head, certain I was in the right. "You never listen. If you listened, you would've been here on time."

"If I listened to everything you said, I'd still be sitting on the other side of town waiting for you." He downshifted to pass a car, the fingers of his hand deliberately grazing my knee. "You specifically said Belmont. I've got the text message. Do you want to see it?"

"No." I crossed my arms over my chest and huffed, unwilling to concede he might be right.

"So how'd your interview go?" His hand left the gearshift to caress my thigh. I felt an instant rush of heat up my leg and into my center.

"It was good, I think." I frowned, mentally running through the course of the meeting. "I don't know. How about you?"

"Good," he said, but from the tone of his voice, I knew he was holding something back. I tensed, the backlash of our previous issues rearing their ugly heads. Although the last week had been relatively uneventful, we were still finding our way around each other, walking on eggshells. He shot another sideways glance at me, filled with heat and strength, the kind that made me rub my thighs together to soothe the internal itch. "I closed on the Chicago apartment and the office too."

I eased my fingers around his, knowing how big a step he was taking. He'd built an empire and lost it, and Sam never liked to lose. His life was about to change drastically. I studied his profile, the squared jaw, the high cheekbones, and stubborn chin. He looked younger, more relaxed than I'd seen him since our reunion.

"I'm sorry, Sam," I said softly.

He lifted my hand and placed a kiss on the back of it. The heat of his breath on my skin sent a ripple of gooseflesh up my arm. "It's fine, baby," he said. "I'm good."

"Really?" I disentangled my hand from his and reached across the car to brush his hair back from his forehead.

"Really." The genuine light in his eyes eased my worries.

"You wouldn't hold out on me, would you?" I wrinkled my nose, thinking of how fragile the trust was between us. One slip, one omission, could end this relationship for us. "I mean, if something's wrong, you'll tell me. Promise me."

"I promise, Dakota." His deep voice held a note of irritation, but his gaze held nothing but desire. I liked to challenge him at every turn. Guys like Sam needed to be kept off balance, and I planned to do my best.

The following week, Sam arrived at my apartment a little before sunset with Chinese takeout and a movie. I loved watching him move around my kitchen, overtly male and overpowering in my tiny space, banging cabinet doors and searching through the drawers for utensils. He wore faded blue jeans and a short-sleeved Henley, items I'd chosen for him on an impromptu shopping excursion. He looked at home, like he belonged there.

After dinner, I watched him rinse off his plate in the sink. Tears of happiness stung my eyes. I wasn't sure how this had all come about or when things had changed. Neither of us talked about the future or the direction of our relationship.

We hadn't had sex, wanting to prolong the newness of being together, to reconnect on an emotional level before getting physical again. For the first time, it was enough to just be together, to just *be*.

Sensing my gaze upon him, he looked up. Our eyes met. He stopped, plate in hand, hovering in midair. I felt the weight of his gaze travel over me, saw his tongue sweep over his lower lip, heard the heavy exhale of his breath. The heady jolt of attraction surged into my center. I placed a hand on my belly to calm the fluttering inside.

"Dakota." There it was. That one word. My name. The way he said it, deep and low, made my breath hitch.

"Yes?" His eyes hadn't left mine. My mouth went dry. I tried to swallow.

"Come here." He set the plate into the sink and came around the counter.

My heart rate accelerated, blood plummeting through my veins. I recognized the tone of his voice and what it meant. I walked to him until we stood toe to toe and looked up into his eyes. They were dark, hooded, and liquid as they traveled from my lips to my breasts and back up again to my eyes. "Sam?" I placed a hand on his chest, surprised to find his heart thudding as hard as mine.

"I want you," he said. Three simple words. They held a million different meanings, a million possibilities. My mind skipped through each one, trying to decode his thoughts.

"I want you, too," I whispered.

He rested his forehead against mine and ran his hands over my bare arms from shoulder to wrist. We swayed together to silent music. I enjoyed the mingled heat of our bodies. His big hands went to my waist and gently lifted me into the air. I wrapped my legs around him and let him carry me toward the bedroom.

After he set me down, his hands drifted over my breasts, thumbing my nipples through the cotton of my T-shirt. They drew up into tight nubs. He bent and sucked one into his mouth, his breath hot and wet against the material. I moaned, unprepared for the instant bolt of pleasure jolting into my core. I dug my fingers into his hair. He looked up at me, eyes filled with emotions I couldn't identify, then stood to kiss me again.

"I've fucked you a hundred times," he said, his voice hoarse. "But this is different."

"Yes." I slipped my arms around his neck and held him close, savoring the warmth of his body next to mine and the sensation of being safe. I knew he'd always protect me, always have my back, through the best and worst of times. We'd already been through hell and come out on the other side, singed but still together.

"If you ever leave me again, I won't make it," he said. The tremor in his voice tore my heart into tiny pieces. Inside my big, strong man lurked an insecure boy who just wanted me to love him. "Promise me you won't leave."

I took his face between my hands and stared into his eyes, willing him to understand. "I promise."

His fingers threaded into the hair at the nape of my neck and pulled my head back, exposing my throat. He dropped soft, hot kisses from my jaw to my collarbone. My pulse fluttered where his lips lingered, sending rapid bursts of adrenaline through my body. I struggled to move, but he held me against him, easily overpowering me, always gentle.

"One of these days, I'm going to tell you I love you." He nipped the tender flesh beneath my ear. I clenched my thighs together to stave off the burgeoning ache between them. His murmured words drove me crazy, made me wriggle with need.

"I'll say it back," I said, choked by the power of his confession. "I've already said it." I bucked against him, impatient to have him inside me.

"Sweet," he whispered. "My Dakota. Mine."

"Always," I replied, thrilling at his words.

His hands left my hair long enough to drag my sweats down to my ankles. I kicked them off, drawing my T-shirt over my head at the same time, eager to get on with the business of making love. He pulled off his shirt, revealing taut abs and the trail of dark blond hair leading beyond the waistband of his jeans.

I sucked in a breath, always overwhelmed by the sight of his naked beauty. We moved onto the bed together. I inched backward on my elbows while he crawled over me, graceful and predatory. His knees nudged apart my thighs. I opened for him, willing and eager. When his fingers slipped between my legs, I was slick for him.

"So wet. So ready," he whispered against my mouth. He fumbled in the nightstand for the foil packet. We'd done this so many times before as husband and wife. And now we were doing it again, divorced but together.

"See what you do to me?" I said as I watched him roll a condom over his erection.

He gripped it by the base and grinned back at me. "See what you do to me?" he replied.

We didn't speak again for a long while. He covered me with his hard body, centering his cock at my opening. Our gazes locked together as he slid into me, one inch at a time. The sweet, agonizing pleasure of it robbed me of all speech. I watched his face, mesmerized by the tiny twitches of muscle in his jaw as he slipped in and out of me.

It was worth it. The heartache. The pain. I'd do it all over again for one night like this with him, to hear his grunts of ecstasy, to enjoy the wiry hairs of his thighs against my legs. The way his hands clutched my breasts, the way he shifted my pelvis to intensify the friction between us, deepen the angle. Our love had nearly ruined us, yet it was the most beautiful thing I'd ever known.

Chapter 38

Dakota

AUGUST ARRIVED WITH a blast of heat, but Sam and I were still together. I sat at the picnic table in my mother's garden with Rockwell across from me and Crockett on my left. I had to wonder how we'd gotten here, to this place, from where we'd been. Sam sauntered from the kitchen, a plate of steaks in his hands. I smiled at the sight of him, experiencing the same tingles and jolts I'd experienced the first time we'd met. He was wearing faded blue jeans, a pinstriped dress shirt untucked with the sleeves rolled up, and a baseball cap. My mom followed with a tray of potato salad, baked beans, and her special broccoli casserole.

"Smells great," Rockwell said. "You're going to make me fat, the way you feed me."

Mom patted him on the shoulder. "We'll see."

Crockett rolled his eyes, catching my gaze and smiling. He looked good. The apples of his cheeks were pink from too much sun, and he'd cut his hair into a bristly crew cut. For the first time in years, his blue eyes were clear and bright. "Can we eat now? I'm starving."

Sam folded his tall frame onto the bench beside me, his hand finding mine beneath the table. We'd come a long way over the past few weeks. We went on dates, fought about everything and nothing, just for the pleasure of making up.

After dinner, I helped Mom do the dishes while Crockett, Rockwell, and Sam sat outside and argued about sports. I watched them through the kitchen window. That was when it hit me. I was happy, truly happy, for the first time in years.

"Can I steal your helper?" Sam eased up behind me, wrapped his arms around my waist, and planted a kiss on my neck.

I shivered, enjoying the warmth spreading through my veins at his touch.

"Sure. Get out of here." My mom waved a hand at us. "Rockwell will help finish up. Won't you, Rockwell?"

He nodded ascension. By the way his blue eyes drank in my mother, he regarded the request as a privilege. Before the door closed behind me, I caught a glimpse of Rockwell pressing a kiss to my mom's cheek. Pure bliss exploded inside my heart.

Sam and I walked down to the lake, holding hands, not talking. When you're really comfortable with someone, the spaces between words can be as telling as the words themselves. It was that way with us. I knew he had something on his mind by the way his jaw tightened every few minutes. He skipped a few stones across the water, watching the concentric rings ripple and fade, before finally speaking.

"I think we should buy a house together," he said.

I found a smooth, flat stone at my toe and handed it to him. "With what? Your good looks?" I asked. "You know I don't have any money." I had a new job, but the pay was less than exceptional.

"I've got some money put back," he said, casting a sideways glance at me.

"I thought you were broke." I raised an eyebrow at him.

"Define *broke*."

"Broke is looking for change in your car to buy groceries. Broke is hocking your stereo to pay the rent."

We started walking again, farther around the bend of the water toward a fallen willow tree.

"I might have overstated the situation," he said. "Broke to you and broke to me are two different things." He let the stone fly, and I cheered when it hopped a total of five times before plopping into the depths.

"Exactly how much money do you have socked away in your piggy bank?" I teased.

"About ten million, give or take."

We'd reached the willow tree by then. He sat down on the fallen trunk and pulled me onto his lap. I tried to squirm out of his embrace, laughing, but he held me tighter.

"Are you kidding me, Seaforth?"

"No." The grin on his face lit up my heart in a way I hadn't known possible. "It's not much, but it's enough to give us a start with a new business. One that we can run together."

"Are you offering me a job?" A flutter started in my belly when he ran the tip of his nose along the side of mine. "Because you know that didn't go so well last time."

"Yes, I'm offering you a job, and a home if you want it."

"I'd like to pay for my half," I said in a wavering voice, distracted by the tiny kisses he peppered along my collarbone.

"We'll see," he murmured. "Reach in my breast pocket. I've got a present for you."

Excitement heated my cheeks. He was always doing little things for me, bringing flowers, writing love notes and putting them on my refrigerator, or sending sweet texts in the middle of the day. I dug into his pocket and pulled out a small blue velvet box. I pried it open and there, nestled inside, was my wedding ring.

"Where did you get this?" I searched his eyes in surprise, finding mischief and admiration in their depths.

"I'll never tell," he said, but then the smile fell from his lips. He took the ring from its resting place and held it in the air, pinched between thumb and forefinger. "You are the most frustrating, infuriating person I've ever met. I told you once that I never know whether to spank you, fuck you, or strangle you, and I meant it. But I hope I have a lifetime to figure it out." I swallowed down the lump in my throat, remembering those very words during our first meeting in his conference room. "I gave you this ring once before because I loved you. I'm giving it back now because I still love you. More than ever." His voice softened. "Marry me, Dakota. Again."

EPILOGUE

Sam

A SOFT RAP on the door tore my concentration from the computer screen. I rubbed the sting of overuse from my eyes. From the second-floor landing, the grandfather clock charmed an elegant reminder of the time. Midnight. I had no idea it was so late.

"Can I come in?" Dakota's quiet voice floated on the silence.

"Sure." I minimized the computer screen and watched her walk across the room. God, did she have any idea how she affected me? The way her smile wrenched my insides? "What are you doing up?" I asked. "Do you have any idea what time it is?"

"I know exactly what time it is," she replied. "Do you?"

Her gaze connected with mine, locking me in, pulling me away from thoughts of work. I'd begun to look forward to her outfit each day, to see what tantalizing dress or blouse she might wear. Tonight, a straight green skirt hit just above her bare knees, showing a stretch of tanned, toned calf. When did she have time to sunbathe or work out with all the research I'd piled on her? I held my breath as she came around the desk, swiveled my chair to face her, and rested my palms on top of my thighs. She bent down to look at the computer monitor, and when she did, I caught a peek at the tops of her breasts. My heart did a ridiculous dance inside my chest.

"What are you working on?" she asked.

"Nothing now," I replied, grateful I'd sent the computer to sleep before she got here.

"Poor Samuel. All work and no play." She affected an adorable pout.

With her standing only a foot away, I caught a whiff of her perfume--gardenias, lilacs, and honey--sweet and understated. Her bare arm brushed my shoulder as she straightened, sending a vibration of awareness down my arm.

"You're one to talk," I said. "You should've been in bed hours ago."

"Someone had to stay up and keep you in line," she replied. "Which I'm beginning to find is a full-time job." Her gaze roamed my face, lingering on my eyes and lips. "You look tired." Even after five years of re-marriage, she had a way of seeing through the mask of my defenses unlike any other person. "Let's go to bed."

"I'm not done yet," I said, thinking of all the income statements and projections still requiring my attention.

"Why do you wear a necktie?" she asked, ignoring my statement. "You always hated them." As she spoke, she straddled my thighs and took a seat on my lap. Her fingers slid along the length of the tie from the tip to my neck. She loosened the knot then pulled it from my collar with agonizing slowness. The silk hissed against the linen of my shirt. Hot blood churned through my veins.

"Because my job requires it."

"Bullshit." She released the top of button of my collar, then another one, and another one. I shivered as her fingers brushed the hair on my chest. "You're the boss here. You can wear anything you want."

When I'd married Dakota the first time, she'd been a girl, little more than eighteen. When I married her the second time, she was all woman, racy curves and feminine features. I watched her breasts rise and fall with each inhale, wondering if I should slip a hand beneath her skirt or leave her to explore a little longer.

"Haven't you ever heard of the term dress for success, Mrs. Seaforth?"

"Why, yes, Mr. Seaforth. It's my mantra." By this time, she'd unbuttoned my shirt to the waist. She ruffled her fingers through my chest hair. My cock twitched behind my zipper, awakened by desire.

"Is there anything I can help you with before I leave?" she asked. Her cool, blue-green gaze connected with mine. I tumbled headlong into the depths of her irises, seeing a reflection of myself in the inky blackness of her pupils. She rocked her hips, grinding down onto my growing erection.

"I can think of a few things." In fact, all I could think about was her pouty lips wrapped around my dick, the rough smoothness of her tongue, and the wet heat of her mouth. I never really thought she enjoyed going down on me, though, and I certainly wasn't about to ask.

"Jesus, Sam." She palmed my erection between us. "That's got to hurt."

"It's a little uncomfortable." I'd been semi-hard since our meeting earlier in the day, a tidbit of which I was sure she was aware, given her silent flirtations during the conference call.

She pushed away from me, spreading my knees with her hands, and kneeled between my thighs. One corner of her mouth lifted in a mischievous smile. I couldn't look away from her, mesmerized by the concentration on her face as she lowered my zipper. Her hand slipped inside my boxers to withdraw me.

"So big," she murmured. "You always were an overachiever." She curled her fingers around the shaft and stroked from base to tip.

"Damn, that's good," I whispered, relishing the warmth of her familiar touch.

I watched as she bent and wrapped her lips about the head of my cock. A ripple of gooseflesh started at the base of my spine and radiated up my back. When her tongue swirled the circumference of the tip, it set my skin on fire. I leaned back in the chair and closed my eyes, losing myself in the sensation.

The next time I opened my eyes, it was to watch her deep throat my entire length. I fought to keep from thrusting into her. Instead, I fisted both hands in her hair and gave a tug. She moaned, a quiet, sexy little growl that reverberated into my balls.

"If you keep that up, I'm not going to last," I managed to rasp out. She responded by dragging her teeth lightly from tip to base and back again.

Damn, she felt good. I pulled the pins from her hair and watched it fall forward onto my stomach. While she teased me, I took a long strand of her hair and let it slip through my fingers, trying to think about anything but the molten lava igniting my veins.

She moved back, releasing my cock from her mouth with a little *pop*. "Good. I don't want you to last. I want you to come, Samuel."

The way she said my name with her swollen lips, red from sucking me, and her doe-eyed gaze peering up at me from my lap--it twisted me into knots. Tension tightened the muscles of my thighs. The good kind of tension. The kind that made my bones ache with the need for release. She squeezed the base of my cock with her hand while swirling her tongue around the head. I thrust my hips upward, needy grunts slipping from my throat.

"Not here," I said, summoning all my self-control to speak. "Upstairs. In bed." She tugged on my erection. Hot desire prickled along my legs. "Are the kids asleep?"

"Yes." She paused long enough from torturing me to speak. "So you'll need to keep it down. You know how noisy you get."

"I do not," I protested, then moaned in direct contradiction of the statement. "Come here, woman." I wrapped my fingers around her biceps and pulled her onto my lap. She was pantyless and slipped onto my cock with a moan of her own. "We'll see who makes the most noise."

We eased into a quiet rhythm, backlit by the blue light of the computer monitor. I'd never get tired of this, of her, of our life together. Every time was like the first time, and each time was better than the last. I'd spent ten long years without her. I'd never get those years back, but I'd spend the next ten years making up for it. My pretty, broken girl wasn't broken any longer. --THE END

Printed in Great Britain
by Amazon